RED LACE DIARIES

SD Syns

VINCI BOOKS

Vinci Books

vinci-books.com

Published by Vinci Books Ltd in 2026

1

The publisher and the author have made every effort to obtain permissions for any third party material used in this book and to comply with copyright law. Any queries in this respect should be brought to the attention of the publisher and any omissions will be corrected in future editions.

A CIP catalogue record for this book is available from the British Library.

Paperback ISBN: 9781036702564

The EU GPSR authorised representative is Logos Europe, 9 rue Nicolas Poussion, 17000 La Rochelle, France contact@logoseurope.eu

Scout Thorne

The Secret Tomb

Murder of Crows

Shifter Days, Vampire Nights & Demons in Between

Twisted

Lady Hawk and Her Mountain Man

Hidden Shifter

Wolf

Wolf Retreat

Night Hunter

The Fixer

Kai

Lee

Flynn

Jude

More from N Gray writing as Natalie Michaels

Steve Campbell Psychological Suspense Thrillers

The Last Girl

The Bone Forest

The White Dahlia

I See You

Death in the City

www.ngraybooks.com

A Quick Note

This story contains content that might trouble some readers, including, but not limited to, depiction of and references to murder, sexual assault, violence, and gore. Please be mindful of these and other triggers; practice self-care before, during, and after reading.

This book is set in South Africa. Therefore, it follows UK English spelling and punctuation conventions. Words like colour, neighbour, mouldy, realisation, are not spelling mistakes.

Also, Joburg is an acronym for Johannesburg.

Enjoy!

Part I

Chapter One

Dear Diary,

I'm finally home.

I'm out and feeling more alive than ever. I've also moved back to my hometown. It doesn't feel like I've been away for so many years since not much has changed. I still can't believe how little things have changed since that day.

The house I bought feels similar to the one we owned back when I was a kid. The home we enjoyed playing games in. A home that used to be safe. I loved living there before the screaming started, before the fights, before we had to pack in a hurry, never to return.

But… there's something else about this new house; perhaps it's the size of the rooms, the carvings on the wooden doors or the air that flows through it; whistling a tune from back then. It's me the walls call to, even though it sounds impossible; absolute madness, but I know something is there as it draws me deeper into the abyss.

A strange feeling washes over me as goosebumps spread across my skin. Then, just as quickly, it disappears, and I feel at home again. It's hard to explain. It's a strange sensation. I come alive with it.

"Right," said the contractor. "We've set up your washing machine and dishwasher, and both are working perfectly. We've painted the walls outside, the walls inside," he raised his arms to show off their work, "everything you wanted us to do is done, on time, and to your specifications." He smiled a toothy grin.

"It looks great, thank you," I said, relieved I didn't have to do any of it myself. "And you guarantee the paint will last at least five years?" I arched an eyebrow.

"Yes, ma'am. Even in this humid weather."

I handed over proof of payment. "Your boss said I can give you this upon completion."

"Thanks," he said, taking the piece of paper and waving it. "We'll get out of your hair so you can settle in and enjoy your home."

"Miss," a tiny woman yelled as she ran down the stairs, her eyes wide and skin pale. She was so short she stood under my armpit. Even though she was petite, she was a hard worker who used the stepladder more than anyone.

"What's wrong, Mavis?" I asked as panic fought its way to the surface. I'd never seen Mavis so scared before.

"It's upstairs, Miss, on the third floor." She pointed up. "There's something there, but I can't see it. None of us can."

"What do you mean?" I choked on the last word, fear gripping me, squeezing my throat tightly as I hurried towards the stairs.

She shrugged. "I don't know," she said, glancing up. "It's heavy and dark, and it scares me. Mpho doesn't want to clean there anymore." She exhaled audibly. "We've cleaned everything; we dust, we vacuum, we wipe. Everything looks good." She was born in Malawi and worked legally in South Africa for years, but every now and then I heard her Malawian accent come through.

"Okay," I said. My voice quivered as I ascended the stairs one at a time; I needed to understand what she was going on about but at the same time not. It was something I'd felt too, but thought it was just me. If Mavis and Mpho sensed something too, I might not be as safe here as I'd hoped.

Mavis walked beside me, visibly shaken.

"Tell me again. Did you see something, or was it only a feeling?" I asked, remembering the first time I'd walked through the house, feeling something, too. I had struggled to cross the threshold of that last step on the third floor, but after that day I felt nothing.

"Yes," she shook her head, "it makes all the hair on my body stand up." She rubbed her arms for effect.

We climbed the stairs together. When we reached the third floor, I stopped on the last step. Darkness flooded the corridor, surrounding us with shadows so thick I couldn't see past my hand. I glanced at Mavis, but she too disappeared behind a blanket of blackness.

Blood rushed to my ears, and ice moved throughout my body. A cold sweat covered my skin. Dark shadows covered the hallway. The shadows moved into the two bedrooms and then disappeared into an inky nothingness. Even though there were no curtains on the windows, there was no sunlight cascading in from the outside.

"Are the windows open?" I asked, blinking, my vision clearing. I turned towards Mavis again, and she materialized in a cloud of whiteness. She stood to my left, gripping the banister.

"Yes," she said, nodding, not tearing her eyes away from the corridor. "Everything is open, yet no sun."

I nodded. "Strange."

"This house has bad juju, Miss. There's something else living here with you, and it's not human."

I swallowed hard at Mavis's words.

"We only felt it now when we were done cleaning," she said.

Scraping sounds of metal on metal echoed down the corridor. My heart thumped in my chest as my breathing labored. Something was coming out of the one room. The scratching sound of metal being dragged on dirty floors sent shivers down my spine like a knife through flesh. I stepped down a step so I could get away, and grabbed Mavis's hand to pull her back with me.

"It's okay, look," Mavis said, pointing. "It's just Mpho."

I wiped a stray tear from my cheek as Mpho appeared, dragging a bucket behind her. I breathed a sigh of relief. When she saw us, she pulled on the rope tied to the bucket handle and picked it up.

As Mpho traversed down the corridor, splinters of sunlight cascaded in through the windows of the bedrooms, brightening the area.

"It was spotless before we started," Mpho said with a deep frown.

"What do you mean?" I asked, the lines between my brows deepening.

"There was nothing for us to clean."

"I don't understand. The contractors worked here and didn't clean up after themselves." They first had to scrape the paint off the walls and then paint again; it's what we'd discussed and they'd agreed to.

"No, ma'am," the contractor said behind us, making me

flinch. I hadn't heard him following us. "We didn't have to paint. The two rooms here were spotless when we checked, so we left them. We didn't quote you on it either."

"Oh," I said, feeling unsure about whether I'd seen them paint up here or not, and that I was sure the rooms needed a fresh coat of paint and the floors needed cleaning.

I'd fallen in love with this house the moment I walked through the front door. But as I'd traversed the corridors, I'd felt something strange, and perhaps that strangeness was happening right now, because I was sure these two rooms were dirty when I'd moved in. The house had stood empty for years; it was dirty everywhere. It's possible that I'd been so busy with the chaos of the contractors, movers, and cleaners that I hadn't checked properly.

"What about the windows?" I asked.

"Someone had bolted them shut. We tried prying them open, but they wouldn't budge. Nothing can get in or out of the third floor," the contractor said. "We didn't want to break anything, so we left it alone."

"Thanks," I said, grateful he'd thought ahead.

"Come, boys!" I flinched when he yelled. "Let's go. We have another job to do." Footsteps echoed as his workers came out of the rooms they were busy in and ran down the stairs, carrying their belongings. "Bye, miss," he said, waving over his shoulder as he traversed down the stairs two at a time.

"We go now, too," Mavis said as she descended the stairs with Mpho following her.

I didn't want to be the only one still standing there, so I followed them to the ground floor.

The removal company and the contractors were busy leaving while I paid Mavis and Mpho for cleaning the house. The removal company I'd used was heaven sent.

They unloaded all my belongings I'd kept in storage while a handful of ladies helped unpack everything. All I had to do was direct which box needed unpacking in which room. It wasn't much to unpack, but not having to do any of the work myself was a weight off my shoulders and allowed me the time to deal with the contractors.

"We see you in two weeks' time?" Mavis confirmed for the fifth time.

"Yes, please, come back in two weeks," I said, holding up my index and middle fingers. "I don't think I can clean this big place all by myself."

"Then why did you buy? It's too big a house just for you," Mavis said, stuffing her money in the top of her bra for safekeeping.

I stared at her as if she'd sprouted a third head. I couldn't answer her question. "You know, Mavis, I don't know why I bought this monstrous house for myself. What I do know is, the moment I stepped inside, I knew I was home. I love it. I mean, what's not to like? The house is an antique, yet it's modern and spacious. And apart from the marvelous sea views, it feels like home to me. You know?"

"No." Mavis' frown deepened. "I don't understand why some white folk do what they do, but it's okay," she said while packing her bags. "We see you in two weeks."

"Okay," I said. "Thanks for coming at such short notice."

I smiled as the two women left. Mavis was honest and seemed to be one of those people who did what she wanted and when she wanted to, which I respected.

When everyone had left and it was only me in the house, the silence stretched and yawned, filling me with a heavy stillness. I turned around in the foyer to look up the staircase, the living room on my left, then the kitchen ahead of me.

This was mine. This was my home.

The tightness I'd felt in my chest eased, and I could breathe again.

Tonight would be my first night in the house. The first evening of the rest of my new life.

Earlier when I went to the shop I'd bought enough groceries to last me the week and as I went to pay; I'd grabbed a few magazines; I wanted enough reading material to keep me occupied while I settled in with my new surroundings without having to go again.

I wanted to take the time to get to know myself again without the doctors or counsellors telling me what I had to do and at what time. I no longer wanted to follow a schedule. After being in rehab for two years, I wanted to ease into the world again, and at my pace.

Perhaps I could find a man who would accept me; and that meant *everything* about me. My life hadn't been as wonderful as most, but I was determined to make it mine again. And the time was now.

Sadness enveloped me, and I huddled into myself when another chill caressed my shoulders. It had been a while since any man had held me. I craved the warmth and touch of his large hands on my body. I yearned for flesh on flesh, along with the desires and sensual play that accompanied it. And I wanted all of it. Then when we were ready, we could have a child of our own.

That was my biggest wish. I desperately wanted a child.

After everything I'd been through, one would think it was the last thing on my mind, but it's not. It's something I'd always dreamed of, and I could only hope I'd be as great a mother as mine was. She'd done everything in her power to protect me. And I missed her dearly. I wished she could see me now. I wanted her to be proud of everything I'd accomplished.

The antique chair on the balcony in my room came with the house. I couldn't wait to sit there and write in my diary. The beautiful scenic views of the ocean and town could fuel my writing and help me establish a routine I was comfortable with. And in my diary, I wrote my secrets, thoughts and desires that I'd carried for years, waiting for release.

I had many desires, and an appetite that needed sating.

And every morning I would wake up to breathtaking views from both of my windows. The water was majestic in all its splendor, with a private path from my back door leading down to the beach.

Yet, as I sat in my balcony chair now and watched the water, something tugged at my very being because of the only thing wrong with the house.

The third floor.

That perhaps the house was telling me I shouldn't be here—and the house wasn't really mine.

Dear Diary,

It's been two days since moving into my new home. Everything had been fine until this morning when I awoke with a terrible weight on my chest. It felt as if someone was sitting on me; I struggled to move and could barely breathe. It didn't matter how I twisted and turned my body; I couldn't get out from under that weight.

After a few short, shallow breaths, the weight eased, and I could take my first deep breath. I kicked the covers off as if that caused the pressure on my chest. My clothing stuck to my skin, leaving me feeling dirty and in desperate need of a shower.

While I showered, I thought about my dream, but I couldn't remember much of it, yet I felt awful; stained from the residual left-over that was dark and evil.

After my shower, I couldn't go back to sleep just yet, so I sat on my balcony and watched the cerulean sea until the sun rose, and I was ready for my first cup of coffee.

I read through a magazine, tore out a few articles and ads about touristy things I might like when I was ready to venture outside again.

Then, as I stood up to go to the bathroom, I heard something on the third floor…

I stood in the middle of my bedroom and listened to… sounds… scratches… something. I steadied my breathing and closed my eyes; it sounded like someone calling a name, or it was the wind squeezing through windowpanes creating ominous sounds.

The lines between my eyes deepened as I walked to the door and listened again.

Silence, except for my breathing.

I traversed up the stairs to the top floor to see if the noise started up again. When I stood on the last step; nothing. Dead calm. The sun cascaded through the windows with its golden glow. All the hair on my arms stood on end.

Even though I awoke early, I had a lazy day. It was late afternoon, and I'd only eaten a slice of toast with peanut butter on it and a banana. I entered the kitchen and started chopping vegetables to make a salad for dinner.

Once done, I sat at the kitchen table and ate while I

leafed through a different magazine. I'd already read two magazines cover to cover, and this one boasted more information on the seaside town I now called home.

I rinsed my plate in the basin and left it on the drying rack and walked through the house. A smile stretched across my face as I thought about *my* house. I'd bought it with the money my mother had left me after she died. It had earned enough interest in these last two years while I was in rehab that I never had to work.

I trailed a finger over the smooth white wall of the foyer until I stopped at the stairs and glanced up at the various floors. On the first floor was my large spacious room and a bathroom with breathtaking sea views. The second floor was the entertainment area; I'd bought a second-hand pool table that fitted perfectly on one half of the room, and a comfortable couch against one wall of the other half, with a large flat screen television on the opposite wall to the couch. Then there was the third floor; a floor that made my arms pebble.

I blinked slowly. When I opened my eyes, I was standing on the third floor with one foot on the edge of the last step. The darkness flooded the corridor and swallowed me whole. My chest rose and fell as I sucked in deep breaths of air. I wanted to get away, but was momentarily frozen in that spot. I couldn't remember climbing the stairs to get to the third floor. It wasn't a place I wanted to visit regularly. Yet, I was here.

Shutting my eyes tight, the surrounding air moved, and when I opened my eyes again, it was just the same boring corridor. Nothing out of the ordinary.

I stepped down, glad I could move again, and ran down the stairs to my bedroom; slamming my door shut, locking it.

Dear Diary,

After yesterday's minor episode of wandering up to the third floor and not remembering, I stayed in my room for the rest of the day.

I wrote in my diary. I read. Then I wrote some more.

The house was quiet. There were no sounds, nothing calling or reaching out to me. It was comforting. I could relax completely and enjoy my home.

While sitting on my balcony, I watched everyone outside, and it made me sad. I wanted to go outside again, to feel the warmth of the sun against my skin and to enjoy life. As much as I wanted to leave my house, I didn't; that meant everyone would watch me. Their eyes would follow me everywhere. It was a silly thought because nobody knew who I was. Nobody knew I was here.

I had an element of anonymity.

I could be anyone I wanted to be.

Part II

Chapter Two

Dear Diary,

I've been wandering around my new home these last few days, and the walls are closing in on me. The cream-coloured walls are moving like slithering snakes, while the curtains animate before my eyes; it's reached a point where I can no longer take it.

I have to get out and see more of the world I'd forgotten.

I think I'm ready to venture out again.

There's no way I can stay at home for long periods of time without going mad. I've started hearing things; scratches from beyond the walls, soft cries and moaning in the distance.

I must get out before I lose my mind.

There's a local gym within walking distance of my house, and I was thinking of joining. It's a way for me to get out and exercise and possibly meet new people... perhaps... perhaps I'll meet someone special?

His name badge read *Todd*. He eyed me several times while tapping on the keyboard as he added my details. The local gym was one of the biggest in the country and very popular. It was part of a large chain, and for the exorbitant fee, it came with all the bells and whistles, and they ensured members' privacy.

"Right, Miss Beukes, everything is in order with your new membership," Todd said, giving me his winning smile. "Now that you have paid the start-up fee, you only have to continue with the monthly cost to remain a member. Since you are paying cash, don't forget to pay on the first of every month."

"Thank you, Todd," I said, returning the change to my purse. I had to pay over a thousand Rand before they would even consider typing in my details into their system.

"I thought I knew all the beautiful ladies who live here. You must be new to our seaside town?" A large man said beside me. His tailored suit strained against his muscular body. He peered down at me as he removed his sunglasses and flashed a rehearsed perfect smile.

"Yes, I moved to Cape Town from Johannesburg a week ago," I said. "Thought I'd take in the views on a more permanent basis." I moved through the turnstiles as the man handed his gym card to Todd to swipe.

"My name is Neville," he said as he moved in behind me through the turnstile. He was so close I smelled his cologne as he pocketed his gym card and extended his hand.

"Jasmine," I said, shaking his hand. But instead of shaking, he brought my hand to his full lips and kissed my knuckles. "I didn't know men still did that." I smiled.

"I still do it, especially for women as beautiful as you." He didn't hide the fact that he raked his dark gaze from my toes to my breasts where he took his time, then finally at my face. "I'm glad you joined this gym; it's nice and private." He winked.

"I'm sure I'll enjoy it here." I offered him my most seductive smile as he let go of my hand. "Perhaps I'll see you around." I glanced at my surroundings, then back at Neville.

"I look forward to it," Neville said, staring at me with lustful intent until he entered the men's bathroom.

"Miss Beukes," Todd said, approaching me from behind the counter. "It's none of my business, and I apologize in advance for speaking out of turn." Then he leaned forward and whispered. "Stay away from Mr. Neville Adams."

"Oh," I said, my interest piqued. "Why?"

Todd licked his lips as he glanced around, ensuring nobody heard. "He has a certain reputation here, and I would hate for you to be mixed up with someone like him. He may be wealthy, but you have class, and there's a difference, and I wouldn't want him to hurt you."

"Thank you, Todd," I said, patting his hand reassuringly. "I appreciate your concern; I know men like him and will remain vigilant." I smiled; I'd known men like Neville all my life and knew how to protect myself.

"Good." He stood straighter and was almost relieved to hear that I could take care of myself. "Just a reminder that the gym closes at ten tonight, so you have just over an hour left. Luckily, it's empty, so you have the place to yourself." He sat in his chair and picked up the book he'd been reading when I'd arrived.

"Thanks, Todd, I won't forget," I said as another man walked in and offered Todd his card for entry.

At nine in the evening, the gym was empty, which I

preferred. I didn't have to fight for my turn on an exercise machine.

I walked around the counter and headed towards the machine area. Todd was kind enough to give me the deluxe tour before I'd paid and showed me where everything was; the pool, sauna, weight area, the various classes they offered, and lastly the floor where all the machines were.

I went to an elliptical machine in the middle of that row, set my watch on the chosen workout and hit '*Start*' on the machine. I brought my electronic reader with so I could read while I worked out; reading seemed to ease the boredom that came with exercising, and I hated watching those little screens on the exercise equipment. The only entertainment I could view was sports, news, or music videos, and I hardly ever watched television anymore. I preferred to read.

Chapter Three

After about twenty minutes on the elliptical machine and pushing my limits, my legs started burning, and I slowed down. All the hair on the back of my neck stood on end. I felt his gaze sweep over me as if he had already touched me with his powerful hands.

Neville climbed onto the elliptical machine next to mine, already dripping with sweat. He glanced at me with one side of his mouth tilted upward in a sly smile.

"Hope you don't mind if I join you?" he said as he started the machine.

"Not at all." I smiled and continued my workout at a slower pace while reading.

"Is it any good?"

I glanced up at him. "What?"

"Your book?"

"Yeah, it's a paranormal suspense novel with a hint of romance. Do you read?"

"I hardly have the time. It's work, gym, and then home for me."

"You should read while you work out."

"I'm only on this side because you're here." He winked and continued with his workout.

Every so often I would feel his eyes on me as if he were undressing me, one piece of clothing at a time. His biceps and forearms flexed as he squeezed the handle of the elliptical machine, white-knuckling it; I thought he was about to snap it in half.

The sexual tension radiating from him could set a dozen women on fire, and I wondered what his touch felt like. It had been so long since any man had touched me, and as I moved on the elliptical machine, I thought about the last sexual encounter I had, which was over two years ago.

I glanced at Neville out of the corner of my eye again, and he was staring at me.

Waiting.

Pondering.

Needing.

I wanted to feel his hot breath against my neck, then kiss the delicate area between my neck and shoulder. I wanted his powerful hands caressing my body as he explored every inch of me. My breath quickened. My pulse thundered in my ears as I imagined him doing all those delicious things to me. I glanced at his hands, at his thick fingers, and imagined them penetrating my soft core. Then I looked at his soft lips and wondered what they tasted like.

A frustrated sigh escaped my lips as I pictured having someone like him do all those things to my body, and more. And never in my wildest dreams could I have imagined that beside me was a man offering his body to me. I wanted all that he offered. I just wanted one tiny taste to satisfy this craving deep within me.

Even though Todd had warned me about Neville, I still

wanted him. Neville wasn't *the one*. He wasn't the man I'd spend the rest of my life with, but he was someone I could play with tonight, and I would use his body to satisfy my dark hunger.

Flashes of his mouth on mine flooded my vision as one of his hands squeezed my breasts, while the other moved between my legs. I lost my rhythm and almost fell off the elliptical machine.

I flinched when he spoke. "Do you want to join me?" he said.

I glanced at him as I squeezed the handles, ensuring I kept my balance. "Where?" I said, swallowing hard, then licking my lips.

"In the showers," he said, jerking his chin towards the men's change rooms. "I'll give a killer back massage while you rinse off under the hot water." He wiggled his eyebrows.

I was a good girl; thinking naughty thoughts and actually doing them were two different things. In all the years I'd been sexually active, I'd never cheated and never had one-night stands. I'd only thought about doing something as naughty as this but never had.

"It's a very tempting offer—"

"But?"

"I hardly know you." I shrugged. "Besides, I'm not that kind of girl."

He smirked, shrugged nonchalantly, and continued his workout.

The dark need grew stronger.

What was I waiting for? An invitation. I'd been away for a while, was new to the area, and had made no friends yet. He could be my first friend. I had nothing to lose, and I'd changed in the last two years; I was no longer the sweet, obedient girl who did what people told me to do. I was independent, but I also had needs. And this need was growing bigger.

I could do this. I lived only once, and here was this man who didn't seem that bad. He had a toned body, a pretty face, and he wanted me. There was nothing wrong with giving in to my urges this once. And nothing bad was about to happen to me.

Neville was easy on the eye. I imagined running my fingers over his broad chest and taut muscles. He was in excellent shape, and I suspected he could satisfy all my desires if I wanted him to.

"Wait," I said, stopping my machine, "my muscles are sore." I climbed off the machine and rolled my shoulders. Glancing up at him, I smiled seductively.

He stopped his machine, turned towards me, and moved his hand between his legs. "Wait two minutes after I leave and meet me inside," he said, grinning. "I'll have the water running at the right temperature just for you." He climbed off the machine, grabbed his towel, and headed towards the men's bathroom.

Scanning the empty gym, I noted that the man who had entered before I started my workout was there by the weights section. Todd was still reading his book by the front desk, and couldn't see the bathrooms from where he was sitting. Nobody would see me enter the men's bathroom.

I switched off my machine and picked up my bag and towel. I drank some water, wiped sweat off my brow, picked up my reader and placed it in my bag, then I headed towards the men's bathroom.

I heard running water as steam filled the men's change rooms. I traversed down the row of showers towards the one near the end. There were walls that separated each individual shower, but they didn't reach the ceiling, and each had a frosted glass door. I could see Neville scrubbing his arms as I neared. I stopped outside his shower and dropped my bag near the open frosted glass door.

He turned around and looked at me with what I could only describe as hunger in his eyes. Hunger for what lay beneath my sweaty clothing. Hunger for my soft, delicate flesh. Hunger for minutes of pleasure. I kicked off my sneakers and removed my socks. Then, as slowly as possible, I lifted my shirt up and off and threw it on top of my bag. I thumbed the elastic band on my pants, ensuring he watched me attentively. He licked his lips as I slowly pulled down my pants and threw that on my top. I stood before him wearing my red underwear.

"Stunning," he said, stroking his hard cock with one hand and with the other he curled his index finger. "Come here, baby. Now suck."

Neville was beautiful; his toned body was sun-kissed and the same shade all over. His smile reached his blue eyes, and his full lips pressed into a pout—which I assumed he thought would look sexy and seductive—it did not. Normally I would've walked away, but he was attractive enough and he turned me on enough to stay. The need was growing.

I sauntered into the shower and removed my panties, then my bra; dropping them on top of my clothing.

Neville's pupils dilated as he watched me. He held a predatory glare, one that hinted at pleasure and pain.

I neared so I could take over the stroking of his hard cock. The moment I wrapped my fingers around his delicate flesh, his eyes rolled into the back of his head. With my free hand, I caressed his chest, his abs, then trailed my fingers lightly on that inguinal crease, and then around the back to grab his tight ass. His eyes flitted open; his mouth parted.

He gripped my shoulders and pushed me down to kneel before him. I grinned, glanced up at him, and licked the soft tip first, then placed him inside my warm mouth and started sucking as my one hand continued stroking him. I stopped to watch his reaction. When he scowled, I continued sucking harder, and stroking him with my one hand.

A guttural moan escaped his lips. He gripped my head with both hands, using me as his support as he fucked my mouth. His balls tightened when I grabbed them, then started playing with the skin that reached his anus. The combination must've been too much for him. He grunted, pulling out.

"If you carry on like that, I will fuck that pretty mouth and come down your throat." Neville grabbed me under my arms and lifted me up. I wrapped my legs around his waist and my arms around his neck. He pushed me up against the wall and positioned himself near my opening, looking at me for permission to enter. I kissed him in that moment; the taste of his soft lips and bit down. He moaned in our kiss and entered me. "Oh, gods, you feel so good," he said huskily.

"Be gentle," I whispered near his ear. "I haven't been with anyone in a really long time."

Nodding, he took his time; entering slowly until he couldn't go any further. My moist walls engulfed him, and then he slowly started pulling out without leaving me completely. Then he pushed his way inside again and slowly retreated so I could adjust to the length and girth of him; like the waves of the ocean meeting the shore. He continued at that speed until he found his rhythm, and then he started pumping into me faster.

He growled into the nape of my neck and said, "It's time to fuck you like you've never been fucked before." He held onto my shoulders, pushing me deeper onto his cock and against the shower wall, and started pounding into me. Every time he hit the top of me, I whimpered while he grunted in pleasure. I held onto his shoulders and dug my nails into him without drawing blood.

He thrust into me with primal instincts, and I contracted in satisfaction in response to his touch and noises. He pounded without restraint in response to my moaning and pushed inside me one last time. His heat poured within me, and I spasmed around him again.

My body thrummed like a tuning fork from the waves of orgasms. He bit my shoulder and pushed his body against mine and into the wall. He was breathless and trying to keep us both from crashing to the shower floor. I unwrapped my legs from his body, and he gently set me down.

"God, that was," he swallowed, and licked his lips, "something else, Jasmine. Holy shit, but that was one hell of a tight fuck." He kissed me chastely, then turned and started washing himself.

I grabbed the bar of soap from him and lathered it up in my hands, teasingly washing myself while he watched. A sly smile played on his lips. Once I was clean, I handed him his soap back.

"This was great and all, but you understand it was only a onetime thing?" he said coldly, and continued washing with his back to me.

"I know," I said nonchalantly as I rinsed off under the hot shower. Once all the soap was off, I exited the shower, grabbed a gym towel from the nearby shelf and wrapped it around my body.

I returned to his shower and watched. He moved with purpose as he washed himself. He knew I was there, but pretended I wasn't. I understood men like him; I was just an available girl he fucked and would never see again. I couldn't complain because I used him too, but I didn't make him feel the way he just made me feel; cheap; used; a whore.

I was not the first woman he used, nor would I be the last. Men like him went through life using people, using women, without giving us a second thought. He disconnected himself from his actions, including his emotions; but I doubted he had any. And although we used each other, that didn't mean he could continue unpunished.

Just by looking at him, I knew he was here every evening, exercising every muscle. He was a fine, perfect specimen. God's gift to women. He took pride in his appearance, using it to his advantage, and he knew what was between his legs. No other male could compare themselves with him.

Reaching for my bag, I unsheathed my knife. With his back to me, I admired his broad shoulders and all those perfect muscles. It was a shame it came to this, but he needed to be punished.

I trailed a finger lightly down his back. He glanced over his shoulder and smirked.

"Seconds?" he chuckled.

On my tiptoes, I covered his mouth at the same time I stabbed him in his side, piercing an organ. He flinched and cried out into my hand. He gripped my hand tightly, prying it off his face, and turned around. I continued stabbing him as he moved, leaving four large wounds in his abdomen, before he collapsed to his knees, his blue eyes widening with fear. Blood sprayed over my chest, neck and face, drenching the towel. I stabbed him four more times in his chest; his warm blood covered my hands. When I removed the knife from the muscle above his left collarbone, he fell to his hands and stared at the floor as he watched his blood pool beneath him and down the drain.

I removed the towel from my body, grabbed the soap off the floor, and lathered it up to wash my body again.

Neville leaned back, collapsing against the wall. He stared at me in shock, his hands covering the oozing wounds in vain, until he exhaled his last breath.

I left Neville on the floor with the hot water falling over him, mixing with his blood and down the drain. Now he was the one who was nothing. His life-force was literally going down the drain, being discarded like he had done to so many others.

Once dressed, I picked up my belongings and exited the men's bathroom. There were no cameras anywhere inside or near the entrance of the changing rooms. I stuck my head out in search of Todd, but he was nowhere to be seen, nor was he near the front desk. The other person was still busy in the weight section, unaware of my presence.

I ran to the turnstiles and exited the gym a minute after ten.

Chapter Four

Dear Diary,

I did it; I took the plunge and went to the gym. I'd probably go again, but it will be the same time I went tonight, when it was at its quietest.

Right now my heart feels lighter and my head clearer after my workout.

I feel like a new 'me'. A 'me' I haven't seen in a really long time.

But I'm in two minds about what I did. I feel shame, yet am honorable. I helped all women by getting rid of someone like him. He was full of himself, full of pride, and full of evil.

The evil surrounding Neville was too big for me to ignore. He needed to be punished for what he was, for how he treated me.

As I finished washing my body, an unknown force took over, driving me to grab the knife in my bag. A knife I don't remember packing. A force that told me to use it on him. To drown out the evil, and to expel him of his sins.

Then, a calm washed over me at the thought that I had used him for what I wanted, and I took pleasure in his touches and the feel of him. It was wonderful. The last time I had so much fun, felt so alive, was over two years ago.

Euphoria engulfed me, and I wanted to stay in that state of mind.

Even though Todd knew that there were only three people inside the gym; I made sure I left no evidence behind. Knowing that Neville had a reputation, perhaps the police would think someone came back for revenge and not look to me as a suspect. I needed to be careful.

The sea breeze caressed my skin and soul as I sat on the balcony writing in my diary.

I loved my new home. A smile reached my eyes.

After my wonderful evening, I could only hope that tonight I would sleep better.

Part III

Part II

Chapter Five

Dear Diary,

Now that I exercise my body daily, I also need to exercise my mind with calming techniques. I've found that early morning short walks on the beach help clear my head of unwanted thoughts and fill my lungs with fresh sea air.

I enjoy watching others walk their dogs, or surfers go out and ride the waves. Sometimes I sit and watch everyone as I press my fingers into the soft sand.

The sound of the crashing waves has almost become my mantra; breathe in, breathe out.

Since I've been going to the gym regularly, I've been sleeping better and for longer hours. For the last few evenings, I've been sleeping for at least seven uninterrupted hours.

I awoke so refreshed today that I've ventured out for a longer walk on the beach, especially since I have so much energy...

I stood in line and waited patiently for my takeaway coffee from the mobile vendor; there was only one of them on Strand Beach promenade. Luckily, his coffee-making skills were excellent, and I didn't have to wait too long for my delicious hot juice. He said his name was Mike and had kind honey-brown-coloured eyes. I paid for my large cappuccino and told him to keep the change.

On the beach, some people were jogging, others were walking their dogs, and there were even mothers carrying their babies. The air was cool against my face as the wind blew grey clouds above us and blocked the sun. They predicted rain for the day, but only late afternoon. I zipped up my jacket and blew on the coffee before taking a sip; the warm liquid heated my body.

Since the coffee vendor was near the old dock, I started my walk from that side first. The skeletal remains of the dock stuck out of the water like dinosaur bones. The weathered wood was eerily beautiful against the turquoise sea.

Sucking in the sea air steadied my nerves, and my shoulders relaxed. I remembered why I had moved back to the old seaside town in the Western Cape; the fresh air, the open spaces, friendly people, and my folks had taken up residency in the cemetery.

They allowed nobody to walk further than the old dock because it was a protected area; a fence stopped anyone from walking further up the beach. I turned around to walk back when I spotted surfers riding waves, with one surfer still on the beach. He was sitting on his surfboard and smoking weed; the smell pungent as I approached him.

He glanced up at me and smiled lazily. "Hey," he said. "Join me." He lifted his joint in greeting. "You want some?"

There weren't many walkers on this side of the beach,

so we wouldn't be bothering anyone with the smoke. It had been years since I had tried any recreational drugs, so it wouldn't hurt to try them again. Even though I didn't know this man, I could use the company. I hadn't spoken with anyone since the evening I met Neville. At least this way I could get to know some locals. Plus, there wasn't anything I had to do back at my house besides sit or make food.

"Sure, why not?" I sat beside him and took the joint from his fingers and enjoyed a drag, then I coughed, handing it back to him.

"Have you smoked before?" he asked, a mischievous smile playing on his lips that matched his green eyes. His sandy-brown hair curled and framed his face. His tanned skin looked dry, but it was a typical skin of a surfer who was at the beach every single day.

"Not for a very long time."

"Try again," he said, handing the joint back to me. "Now that it's legal, you can do it without getting caught." He chuckled.

I toked on it again and didn't cough this time. The smoke filled my lungs, and a buzz erupted in my head, and my limbs felt heavy yet light at the same time. My eyes widened in surprise.

"Yeah, it's a fast-acting strain, but it's kosher." He shrugged nonchalantly. "Your mind won't bomb out; it just chills you the fuck out." He chuckled again and took the joint from me.

"Why aren't you with your buddies?" I pointed at the surfers in the water; it appeared as if they were teaching a few people to surf.

"Nah, not up to it today. I enjoy taking it easy, you know." He nodded to himself as he stared at his friends.

"We own the surf school," he thumbed at the building behind him, "but I'm more the entertainer than the teacher." He lifted the joint as if to say that's all he did. He supplied the weed, and that was his job.

I nodded in understanding, stretched my legs out in front of me and leaned back on my elbows. My body felt light, my hearing was clearer, and somehow my vision sparkled with clarity. The sand beneath my body was soft, cold, and strangely comforting. I shuddered when a breeze blew against me from the side, spreading goosebumps all over my body.

"Here," he said, handing me his towel.

"Thanks." I took it from him, placing it on the sand and rested my head on his towel.

"My name is Codhi." He held out his hand to shake.

"Jasmine." I shook his hand.

"You have a beautiful name, Jasmine."

"Thanks."

"Do you have a boyfriend?" he said, toking on the joint.

"No, it's just me." He turned to stare at me, his green eyes hinting at naughty activities.

My mind wandered through the delicious memories of the shower I had with Neville, before I taught him a lesson, and wondered what Codhi could offer; if anything.

Would Codhi be the one to keep my insatiable appetite in check now that I was free to explore again? For two years I had to suppress my urges and salacious appetite. Would he be able to sustain me? Could he be the *one*?

My smile stretched across my face as euphoria chose that moment to enlighten me. My body buzzed from the effects of the weed and what it could be like when it was only skin to skin. My core clenched at the possibilities.

Even though I had only just met Codhi a few minutes ago, he was already offering himself to me. Wanting to give himself over to me completely. It was so easy.

Was this what men did these days? Offered themselves to the first pretty lady they met.

Was it always this easy? I didn't mind; it would be an enjoyable experience. Plus, I wanted to experience the pleasures of the flesh while under the influence, and curiosity got the better of me.

"What do you have in mind?" I purred with excitement.

"You. Me," he stood up, "and our heavenly bodies." He reached for my hand and pulled me to my feet. "We have the clubhouse all to ourselves." He jerked his chin toward the water. "They will be out there for at least another hour." He chuckled, grabbed my hand and led me towards the surf school clubhouse.

Once we were inside, he locked the sliding door of the clubhouse and led me down a dimly lit corridor. When we reached a bedroom, Codhi grabbed the handle and said. "We each have our own bedroom in case it's late and need to crash. We have our own houses too, in case you were wondering." He chuckled and opened the door. "I'm not a complete waste of space, and even though I do little teaching, I organise fundraisers for the school or the kids who don't have surfboards or a wet suite."

I entered his room, and he locked the door behind me. He grabbed my shoulders, his thumbs stroking my muscles in a circular motion. My arms pebbled at the sensation, and my eyes rolled into the back of my head. I opened my eyes when he whispered near my ear.

"Once we start, everything will be sensitive. A kiss will be deeper, a touch will feel like an explosion of nerve endings; but everything will feel great. I promise. They grow the strain only from the best, and it makes you feel so *good*." He let go of my shoulders and grabbed my hips, forcing me to sway with him as he did a little dance, grinding his body into the back of mine. My skin tingled at his touch as I danced with him, our bodies becoming one.

As our bodies moved together, my mind raced. Glancing around his room, the first thing that caught my eye was the colourful wallpaper that slithered and swirled; confusing me. Panic rose within me. "Is it fine to smoke weed if one takes prescription medication?" I said, sounding dream-like and euphoric as I watched the snakes slither through the curtains and up the walls.

I felt Codhi shrug behind me. "I doubt it, babe. You only had like one proper pull. Just don't overdo the thinking and everything will be fine."

When he let go of me, a chill settled into my bones, and I felt alone; I hugged my arms and waited. He headed for the single bed on the far side of his room. He had one of those white wooden bayside headboards with panels; but the paint had already started peeling off the wood. The blue duvet cover had tears on the side and a few dark patches. His bedside table held an alarm clock, an over-flowing ashtray, and a jug of orange liquid. He lay down still clothed and brought his hands behind his head and stared at me.

"Okay," he said, chuckling. "You got me. I stay here more often than I should. But I look after the place at night." His grin widened, flashing white teeth.

While Codhi was sitting on the beach, I didn't get a good look at his body. Now I did. He was toned and tanned. His abs were visible as he started lifting his shirt up and over his head, throwing it against the far wall where there was already a heap of dirty clothing screaming to be washed.

I shuddered at the thought of how dirty his clothing was at the bottom of the pile. I shook off the disgusting feeling; I was here, and he was willing.

More than willing.

Chapter Six

I slowly climbed out of my clothing and stood before Codhi in my red lace underwear. The weed relaxed me, and my skin felt sensitive. It felt like someone was stroking my skin with a feather, making me shiver.

Codhi watched me with lustful eyes, quickly removing his board shorts, and laying back down again.

"You really don't enjoy doing much, do you, Codhi?"

"Hey, what can I say. At least I'm a catch." He chuckled at his joke as he stroked his dick. At least that part of him worked. "Come see what Daddy has for you."

I burst out laughing. "You are too young to say that." I climbed onto his bed and straddled his waist.

"Yeah, like that," he said, grabbing my hips. "Probably, we like what, the same age?"

"Exactly, there's no way you are my *Daddy*."

"Okay, fine. Come here." He sat up and cupped my face. His fingers were rough, and he smelled like the sea; salty and a little fishy, like he hadn't had a shower with soap in days.

His lips were a little chapped as we kissed, but I didn't mind. His quick tongue darted inside my mouth. While his hands explored my body like he couldn't decide where to touch first.

I pushed him off and rested my hands on his shoulders, keeping him on the bed.

"Ooh, yeah, baby. You like it rough?" He wiggled his eyebrows.

"Not really, but you seem a bit confused on where to start first, so I thought I would help you along."

"Fine by me." A sly smile crept up his face as his green eyes twinkled in anticipation.

I grabbed his wrists and pushed them above his head, picked up the material belt off his floor and tied his wrists to the headboard. He grunted in fearful pleasure and nipped at my breast through the bra as I leaned over to tie his hands.

I sat back and slapped him in the face. "Naughty, don't touch unless I give permission."

"Ooh, yeah, baby, I love role-play," he said.

"Good boy." I sat back, moving my body so that his cock was flat against him and pressing against me. His cock throbbed, and he tilted his hips upward. "So greedy!" I said, slapping his chest. "You lazy, greedy pig." I leaned forward and sucked on a nipple, then the other. I glanced at his face, his eyes closing and his lips parting. His skin tasted like salt as I kissed his stomach and trailed lower. I shifted so that I was comfortable and licked his cock, watching it bounce as his hips moved up; wanting more.

I removed my panties and climbed back on top of him. His eyes opened and widened as he pulled on his restraints. "Aren't you going to wrap it?"

"Why, do you have a disease?"

He shook his head, *no*.

"Don't you want to go bareback?" I said, grabbing his cock before he could answer, hovered just above him and aimed it towards my entrance and slowly sat down.

"No, wait," he said, pulling harder on his restraints but stopped as he filled my soft, moist pussy. "Oh, gods," he gripped the headboard and started pushing himself further inside me.

"That's it," I said. "I want to feel all of you." I moaned as I rode him in a circular motion. "You were right; this feels better. It's intense, very sensitive, and I feel all of you." My body thrummed with sensual pleasure, heightened by the weed. Our skin pebbled as one as if our bodies understood in that moment that what we were doing was right. We were becoming one.

I stopped, lifted my bum up slightly until he was about to slip all the way out and then sat back down again. I did this over and over until I could feel he was just about to explode and stopped. He grunted in frustration. Then, with all the energy I had, I fucked him harder and faster. His headboard smashed against the wall as I pushed into him, over and over. Our bodies melted into one with his cock buried deep inside of me, then he hardened and it sent me over the edge.

"I'm coming," he groaned in satisfaction as he gripped the headboard for one last thrust.

I squeezed my orgasm around him as we both rode that wave of pleasure. I reached for the handle from my bag, and as he opened his eyes, I continued to grind into him. Our orgasms hit us over and over, and I sliced his neck. Blood oozed out of the fresh wound and pulsed over my hand as I kept the blade there, shoving it deeper inside his neck. As his heart started beating faster, more blood pumped out. His wide eyes stared at me in surprise.

"Why—" he said, but I cut him off by slicing his neck until I saw his spine. Blood soaked his old, dirty bedding and pooled on the floor. His glassy eyes stared up at the ceiling. His mouth dropped open.

I climbed off him; his limp dick fell to one side. I wiped my knife clean with one of his shirts from the floor and sheathed it back inside my bag. Grabbing wet wipes from my bag, I cleaned the drops of blood off my chest and hand before it dried. Grabbing more wipes to clean between my legs before I dressed. I tossed all the used wipes into a plastic bag and shoved it into my bag; I would discard them when I got home.

Once dressed, I covered his body with a towel. I didn't want to see his face with that pained and shocked expression. Wrapping my hand in a cloth I kept inside my bag, I unlocked his bedroom door and closed it behind me, wiping everywhere I thought I might have touched.

The clubhouse was quiet as I traversed down the corridor, except the wind chimes were making soothing sounds as the wind blew in from the ocean. The smell of nature from an open window eased my tension. With the cloth still in my hand, I opened the sliding door and closed it behind me.

I followed a path through the sand dunes until I came upon a bench that sat atop rocks overlooking the ocean. There were engravings with initials of lovers and hearts binding them. Sitting on the lovers' bench, I watched the cerulean waves crashing onto shore, which sent shivers up my spine as the wind caressed my skin.

The group of surfers were still out on the water. The

walkers and joggers were still leaving footprints in the sand; only to be washed away with each crashing wave. My skin no longer tingled, so I assumed the little bit of weed I'd smoked was leaving my system.

My time with Codhi was enjoyable, but he was a disgusting, lazy pig and deserved that bloody ending.

Glancing down at myself, I noted a blood splatter on my knee. I grabbed fresh wipes out of my bag and wiped my knee clean and continued searching for any other signs of a struggle. Luckily, I had removed all evidence from my body.

My stomach grumbled.

There was a little coffee shop that offered salads, open sandwiches, pastas, pizzas, pastries and all the coffee one could drink. I'd been there once before and enjoyed their food; which was delicious, and the opulent environment was just what I needed right now. I stood up from the bench and followed the path to the coffee shop.

The bell chimed when I opened the door. A server greeted me, letting me know I could sit anywhere. I headed towards the open seat in a booth in the back. A woman took my order, then helped those who wanted to pay.

"Morning," a man said with a *manager* name tag pinned to his chest. He stood close to my table, wearing a kind smile. "Have you ordered your food yet?"

"Yes, thank you."

"This is the second time you've been in here, isn't it?" He asked. It was eerie that he remembered the number of times I had frequented his establishment.

"That's right," I said, narrowing my eyes.

"I'm familiar with my regulars, so if anyone new enters, they're hard to miss." He smiled kindly.

My smile reached my eyes. "I recently moved up from Joburg."

"Welcome; it's always a pleasure serving a fellow South African." He smiled pleasantly. "We get a lot of foreigners here, too." He winked. "Please let me know if there is anything I can help you with."

"Thank you."

"My name is Christopher, or Chris if you wish." He proffered a hand.

"Jasmine," I said, shaking his hand, but he lingered. His meaty hand clasped mine. I pulled my hand free from his, and he stared at me. His chocolate-brown-coloured eyes stripped me naked with their intense gaze.

"I will be over there if you need anything."

"Thanks." I pulled my cellphone out of my bag and thumbed something, anything, to avoid any more eye contact. He was handsome in a small-town kind of way with his brown hair cut short and parted to one side, those soul-piercing eyes that wanted more, and broad shoulders and powerful arms that could bench press over me. I shuddered as I crossed my legs, thinking of the possibilities with *him*.

I should've felt bad for thinking about another man so soon after Codhi, but Chris was hard to miss, especially since he needed to introduce himself to me. Perhaps I could get to know Chris better, and on a deeper level. Anything was possible.

My server approached with my open sandwich; halloumi, avocado, and rocket. She placed the large cappuccino to one side along with the slice of lemon meringue. I was famished and devoured my sandwich, then took my time with dessert. I pulled the device out of my bag and continued reading Deadly Pattern by N Gray.

When I was ready to pay, Chris approached me. "Hope

to see you soon, Jasmine." He purred lustfully and opened the door for me.

"Definitely, and I look forward to it." I cooed and exited the coffee shop.

Chapter Seven

Dear Diary,

I met Codhi today while on my beach walk. He was cute, a typical surfer, but boy was he lazy. While I was with him, something snapped inside me.

I change into this other person; someone I become when the man I'm with behaves in a certain way. My dark need.

I can't describe it. It's a feeling I can't bottle up, and I have to play it out. It all began the moment I moved into this house; I've felt different, good, just very different.

Unfortunately, Codhi was too lazy for my liking. It's no wonder he was easy picking for his bloody demise. I shiver thinking of his warm blood covering my cold fingers as his heart rate kicked up a notch.

One thing I enjoyed about my encounter with him was that I tried weed again. It was the same yet different. It heightened my senses and sent shivers up my spine.

My skin pebbled at the thought of those shifting walls and my sensitive skin when Codhi touched me.

I was lucky enough to leave the clubhouse without being seen and enjoyed breakfast at that cute coffee shop again. I might go there for breakfast every day. And Chris is very cute.

The rest of the day I spent driving around town so I could get a sense of the area. I found a lovely wine estate that offered wine tastings. Found out that there are various hikes up Black Mountain. The hikes start early in the morning so that by the time you reach the first point, you can watch the sun rise.

There's so much for me to do here, and it's a comfort to know that I made the right decision to move back here after so many years. I was so young when we first lived here that I don't remember the area, really.

But where there is good, there is bad, and the size of the house bothers me. There are too many doors to count, and far too many hallways and rooms. To have a three-story mansion all to myself is ridiculous, but I love it at the same time.

It's confusing, even to me.

Part IV

Part IV.

Chapter Eight

Dear Diary,

I struggled to sleep last night.

I opened the French doors to my bedroom balcony, sat on the chair, and watched the moon cascade down on the ocean as its silver tendrils touched the water. The motion of the sea was hypnotic. It was only after an hour that I felt sleepy, and I eventually went to bed.

Then, a ruckus woke me in the early hours of the morning. I could not locate the source of the noise. It may have been a dream that had alerted me to my surroundings, even though there was nothing out of the ordinary.

While I was brushing my teeth, I heard cries from somewhere in my house. It was startling to hear, but I couldn't find where it was coming from. My neighbours are far from me, so it wasn't them. Unless it was someone who walked past my house. My backyard is the beach, so it's understandable that there are people nearby, but it doesn't justify the loud cries so early in the morning.

Once dressed, I'll head out for a wine tasting. There's nothing like the taste of a crisp white wine with the aroma of earthy fruits and flowers in the afternoon, or the medium-bodied allure of an oaky red wine…

The wine estate greeted new arrivals with its large wrought-iron gates. On either side of the gates were iron dragon heads; their eyes followed me as I drove through. Once the gates snapped closed, it looked like a dragon's face in the rearview mirror.

They lined the narrow road leading up to the estate with trimmed hedges and manicured gardens. All the parking spaces were occupied apart from one near the entrance.

Yesterday at breakfast in the coffee shop, I'd heard the women speaking from the table beside me that this was one of the best places to visit and was always full. So when I saw the empty parking space, and so close to the front, I couldn't believe my luck. I parked and sauntered through the beautifully landscaped gardens. A pond with ducks was to the side where families enjoyed picnics, and since the school holidays hadn't started yet, it was mostly couples occupying the grass.

There were strange structures cemented into the grass that, when you held your hand near them, gave off a certain sound. Depending on the shape and size of the structure, the sound changed. An artist had created these magnificent instruments, and I made a mental note of the artist's name; Brandon. The description of the artist told me he was young, and his family owned a large art gallery in New York and Paris, yet he chose South Africa as his home.

I followed the path towards the building for wine tastings and waited in line before being seated. A woman with an umber skin tone, kind eyes, and a wonderful smile greeted me and ushered me towards an open table for two. But before she could show me the way, a large man in a business suit requested that she join the others at a busy table where her colleague required help.

"Allow me," the burly man offered and held the chair out for me. "Are you here for a wine tasting or lunch?"

"The wine tasting, although I am peckish," I said, sitting down as he pushed my chair in behind me.

"Can I offer you the cheese, meat, and biscuit platter for one to complement your wine tasting?"

"Sure, that sounds perfect."

The man nodded and approached the counter to place my order. I glanced around the vast room, which held at least fifty occupied tables. All the customers were in various stages of intoxication and fine dining.

Soon after the manager had left, my waiter arrived and explained the origins of the vineyard and how they processed the wine, along with the various flavours I would taste.

The manager brought the beautifully arranged platter with an array of dry meat, cheeses, biscuits, and nuts. I thanked him and ate some dry meat while I sipped the first delicate wine with a floral aftertaste.

The server returned with the next bottle and a clean glass and explained the process of the new wine. It was smooth on the palate, much like the first, except it had a hint of oak and vanilla. It was a crisp fresh wine I could enjoy any time of the day.

After the third wine, I already felt tipsy and was grateful to have the platter as hunger pains struck at that moment. The tasting of each wine continued until I had tried all four white wines, two rose's and two reds.

Even though I was famished, I tasted each morsel slowly as if I were trying it for the first time. The dry meat complemented the red wine. The cheese somehow went with both the red and the white wines. While the biscuits cleansed my palate so I could taste each of the wines as if I were tasting it on its own with no contamination from the previous wine.

By the time I had finished the wine and the platter, the room was half empty. I had sat there for at least three hours. It's not the sitting alone part that bothered me, but that I had been there for so long and didn't feel time fly.

I drank a glass of water and stood, alerting my server I wished to pay. She neared and told me that the manager would like to speak with me before I left.

"Oh, did he say why?" I asked suspiciously.

"No, ma'am, just that he wishes to see you," she said as she led me down the dark corridor lined with their signature wine bottles to an office at the far end. She knocked and opened the door when he instructed her to do so.

I peered around the corner to find the large man sitting behind his desk, his belly almost resting on top of the table.

"Please come in," he said. His sausage fingers beckoned me near.

I entered and furrowed my brow. "Is there something wrong?"

"No, nothing like that," he said, leaning back in his chair. "I was wondering if you'd like to accompany me on a tour of the cellars?" I arched an eyebrow. "Once a month I choose a customer to walk with me as I go through the routine of checking the wines." He pointed to a wall lined with frames. In each picture, he stood with a customer; be it a man, a woman, a family, anyone he deemed worthy to see the bowels of the winery. "Your meal and wine tasting would be complimentary."

The tension in my shoulders eased slightly, but I remained suspicious. However, I was curious and had always wanted to experience a private tour of this magnitude. "Sure, sounds interesting."

"Great, it won't take long, maybe fifteen minutes at the most." He stood and grabbed his keys.

Chapter Nine

"My name is Scott." He touched my back gently as he led me out of his office. "This way," he said, pointing down the corridor in the opposite direction I had arrived.

"Jasmine," I said, following him down the steps. My arms pebbled at the chill in the air as we descended into darkness. On one side was glass, and below were large metal tanks, which processed the wine before it went into wooden barrels to age.

Scott stopped walking to explain the history of the winery, and that he had been working here for years and would most likely retire here. As he spoke, I looked at him properly since meeting him. He had kind blue eyes, salt and pepper hair that seemed soft like a baby, and his cheeks were round and rosy, with beads of sweat on his forehead. He would be handsome if he lost a few kilograms, but working here was too tempting. All the wine he could drink, all the food he could eat. It was a weight-loss nightmare, and I understood why he looked the way he did.

When his speech was over, we continued walking,

arriving at an underground cellar lined with various wines collected over the years, with a table on one side and a mini-bar fridge beside it.

When we stopped walking, I glanced at his full lips as he spoke. "Upstairs we offer the commercial wines for customers to taste, but down here I offer you the best that we have." He grabbed a bottle of wine from the old wooden shelf and dusted it off. "This one we produced ten years ago. As you will taste, our wines last many years and improve with each passing year." He opened the bottle, grabbed the glasses that sat on top of the fridge and poured one to the half-way mark. He handed me a glass by the stem. "Taste and tell me what you think."

I smelled it first; summer fruits. Then I tasted it. The flavours were complex. At first there was a hint of blue-berry, then the aftertaste of cassis and black-ripe young-berry. Then, once I swallowed, I caught the effects of basil and fresh thyme. "It's very delicious," I said, smacking my lips together, then had another sip. The second time around, I tasted the herbs first.

Scott's smile stretched across his face like a kid at Christ-mas. He poured himself a glass and clinked his against mine. "Congratulations, you just made it onto my wall." He smirked. His dark gaze suggested sinful thoughts as he drank from his glass and stared at me.

On the table he had a handheld camera; which I assumed he used to take pictures of all his lucky clients once they completed his tour.

He regarded me as he drank from his glass. We stood in silence as we stared at each other. He smiled, and it was contagious. I smiled back. An attraction I hadn't expected tugged at my core, and I wondered if he could be the *one* to satisfy my hunger.

Scott seemed genuine and kind, and I couldn't help wondering if he was one of those people who would make me his priority instead of a choice. For a moment, I clung to the fantasy that maybe he really could be the *one*. Someone who would make me feel like I was their world. And make me *feel alive*.

I leaned against the table that held the bottle and loose pieces of paper. I peered up at his blue eyes and smiled, blinking my acceptance of him; my consent. He leaned closer, his lips near mine, hesitating. I welcomed his plump lips, and they were juicy like the wine he had just taken a sip from. When he pulled away, I asked, "Do all your clients get such special service?"

"Only you, my dear," he whispered. He drank from his glass, placed it on the table, and opened the mini-bar fridge door, reaching for a plate of food. "I hope you don't mind. I haven't eaten all day," he said, and started eating before I could answer.

He forked heaped amounts of food into his mouth and barely swallowed before forking another mouthful. He ate the pasta dish cold and finished it shortly after downing his first glass of wine. Then he filled his glass and reached for the fridge again and came back with pizza bread. He offered me some, but I politely declined.

This was a first; I thought we were about to kiss again and get frisky, but then he started eating. While I waited for him to finish, I sipped quietly on the wine and glanced around the cellar while he stuffed his face with food. A sinking feeling hit me then. Just when I had thought this man could have been the one for me, someone I could spend my days with, he had to behave like *this*; someone who couldn't stop eating. He had no *off* button.

"I'm sorry, but I was ravenous," he said with a mouth

full of food. A crumb had fallen out of his mouth and landed on his chin. "When I brought you your platter earlier, I realized I hadn't eaten yet. Then I was busy with other clients and their bookings at the B&B, and by the time you stopped outside my office, I was ready to eat anything." He winked darkly as he shoved another slice into his mouth.

I swallowed the bile that had risen along with my disgust for the man. His forehead peppered with perspiration, and his face flushed. He downed the glass of wine, leaned back in the chair he was sitting in and rubbed his enormous stomach. "Now, can I have you for dessert?" He chuckled with delight, making his belly wobble.

I cringed inwardly, but I knew what I wanted to do with him. He needed to learn his lesson and was a perfect candidate for my punishment. Scott would fit in perfectly with the rest of them on my list. I smiled down at him and gave a curt nod.

"We may play," I said with a wink as that feeling started taking over.

He chuckled lightheartedly and started undressing, his fingers fumbling with the small buttons on his shirt. I closed the door to the cellar and removed my skirt, folding it neatly on the table and placing my bag beside it; I needed what was inside soon. I didn't think Scott would last very long.

I faced the desk, bent over and placed my hands on it, lifting my ass as an offering for him to do with as he pleases. I at least wanted to get some joy before I worked. Glancing over my shoulder at him, but he was staring at my red panties. He licked his lips and grunted in excitement.

"So much I want to do to that tight ass." He placed his sausage fingers on my shoulders and moved in behind me. His hands traced down the sides of my body, grazing the swell of my breast still clothed. He squeezed my waist and went lower over my hips. Then he thumbed my underwear and pulled them down, and I climbed out of them. He picked them up, smelled them before throwing them on my skirt.

"Now where was I?" he said huskily as his one hand caressed down my front and cupped my mound. He moved further down until he found what he was looking for and started rubbing the delicate folds. My head went back automatically as he played with me, sending shivers up my spine. He grunted in my ear. "You are such a fine specimen, Jasmine. I don't think I can last long with you. I will come hard and fast. Are you ready for me?"

In response to his question, I pushed my ass out until his hard cock was between my ass cheeks. "As hard and as fast as you want, lover boy," I said dreamily as he continued teasing me. He shifted himself near my opening, and with a low guttural sound entered me.

He pumped himself deep inside as he held onto my hips. His strength kept me in place as he continued his thrusts. With each savage pounding, I heard him wheeze behind me as his hot breath tickled my neck. Even though he was unfit, he knew what to do with his hard cock as he entered me from behind. He kept changing angles yet still hit that sweet spot deep inside me. His girth was impressive as he filled me and continued his rhythm. Unfortunately, it didn't take him long to reach his peak as the orgasm caught him and then me.

He reached for my receptive little button of pleasure and began teasing it while he continued pushing himself deep within me, which built that sweet pressure, and I came around him again. With one last thrust, he voiced his ecstasy, and then he moved away, pulling out. The sudden loss was evident and left me feeling empty. His hands were still on my shoulders as he tried to catch his breath, and he stood taller, as if he had accomplished something he had always wanted to do.

It was perfect timing.

While he recovered from his exercise, I reached for my bag and bent down so that my left elbow was on the table while my right hand gripped the handle and I moved between my legs. With a flick of the wrist, I sliced upwards. Scott flinched, let go of my shoulders, and grabbed his cock.

I turned around to see his dick hanging loosely by the soft, delicate skin. He crashed to his knees and screamed in pain. His face blanched as he stared up at me like an animal caught in a trap.

I heard him laugh, but I didn't see him laugh. My heart hammered in my chest. Blood pulsed in my ears. He sounded just like *him*. It took me back to a time I wanted desperately to forget. The fear I had once known had resurfaced.

"Why?" Scott cried, sweat dripping down his face as his blood pooled around him.

When Scott spoke, it brought me back into the present. Anger boiled to the surface again, and I remembered why I was here and what I wanted to do.

"Because you are a predator who preys on innocents. How many women have you brought down here and used?" I asked, pointing the blood-soaked knife at his face. "And tell me the truth."

"Not that many," he said, shaking his head. "I never hurt anyone; they wanted to be here with me."

"Did any of them say *no*?"

"No." He sounded insulted.

"Did any of them ask you for a job?"

"Some," a thought crossed his scared face, "I didn't mean to hurt them. They never said, '*no*'."

Visions of the two women's faces in those pictures on his walls flashed before me. The photos where he had his arm draped over their shoulders; they seemed uncomfortable in his embrace and about to burst into tears, or had already cried. If any of those women had wanted a job, I didn't see them here today.

He had used them, discarded them, and they never returned for fear of going through it again and again, day after day. Men like him would use them daily because he got away with it once already.

"You are a predator," I said again. "When did you last look at yourself, Scott?" He just blinked at me. "You disgust me." I kicked him in the shoulder, sending him crashing to the ground. He still held his dick in both hands; his head hit the floor, and his cries echoed in the cellar.

I wiped myself clean, dressed, and picked up my bag. Nearing Scott, his fearful eyes watching me approach, I lifted the blade and swiped down at his neck. A look of confusion splashed across his face. He wasn't sure if he should still hold his severed dick in place, or keep blood from pouring out his neck. But I'd severed two major arteries, and it wouldn't take long for him to bleed out.

The pool of blood filled the cellar floor and was about to touch my shoes. I quickly opened the door and climbed the small step so I left no bloody footprints behind.

I closed the door, wiped it down, and hurried to my car.

Chapter Ten

Dear Diary,

I'm not feeling well.

*Tasting the wines was superb, but the wine tasting tour was a disaster. I met Scott. He was a predator who preyed on naïve women. Most wanted a job from him, and only he could give it to them, but only if they offered themselves to him—*willingly. *He was in a position of authority and used it to his advantage.*

He must have been a handsome man once, but that was long ago. But because of his eating habits, he had become large, lazy, and disrespectful. And I suspected the only time he ever had a woman was when he forced them down in that cellar with him.

Even though there was something about him, there was an evil within that I had encountered before. It took me back to when I was young and innocent and still saw the world as a place where everyone was good and treated you well.

He reminded me of him *so much that I thought I heard him laugh. I tried to push the memory down, but it kept resurfacing... repeatedly.*

I did what I had to do. I severed the part of him he used against those who were weak. Then, before I left, I grabbed a few bottles of wine for my trouble.

I need to sleep better tonight, but my mind still races.

Part V

Chapter Eleven

Dear Diary,

I had another sleepless night.

I don't know what's wrong with me.

I've been thinking perhaps I should go back to rehab? Perhaps living on my own and in this large house isn't the right thing for me; not now.

I think I was wrong to go out; my cravings are consuming me, and I'm afraid there will be nothing left of me once the dark feelings take over.

Since my wine tasting, I've stayed home. I didn't want to leave for fear of seeing someone from the winery, but I doubt anyone saw me leave Scott's office. What bothers me the most is that I don't remember getting home.

Also, I continuously hear scratching sounds within the walls. I've knocked out part of a wall in one of the spare bedrooms only to find pipes. I hear these things, but find old piping, then the scratches continue somewhere else.

I need to go outside again. If anyone saw me do anything, the police should have been here by now.

Shouldn't they?

I need fresh air. I need to get out and explore nature.

I thought I would go for a hike up that mountain and watch the sun rise. Perhaps the exercise and being in the company of others will help me adjust to what I've done. To what I am turning into. Yet, I'm afraid I will do it again.

But the men deserved it. Didn't they?

If I'm to make it in time, I need to leave soon.

I'm dressed in gym clothes and strong sneakers. I don't have any hiking shoes, but if I enjoy today, then I might invest in a pair…

There were a few of us waiting for the mountain ranger, who had agreed to meet us at the starting point. Blocking the entrance stood a group of six young women, all in the twenty to twenty-five age group, all wearing the tightest clothing I'd ever seen. Their hair hung loose around their shoulders, and they wore lots of makeup. I couldn't understand how they could sweat with so much foundation smeared on their skin.

Eyeing one girl, I could see the difference in skin tone versus what she plastered on her face, and it started cracking. Perhaps I was getting old, but no woman should look like that. And definitely not during a hike; there was nobody to impress, especially since we were only women.

I cautiously rubbed sunscreen onto my face, trying to avoid my eyes, and on my forearms. I tied my hair in a low ponytail and pulled on my cap.

"Good morning, ladies," a man said behind us. I flinched and turned to see who it was. The mountain ranger neared and continued speaking. "My name is Timothy, and I will be your guide this morning. I will explain the various fauna and flora as we pass them, but if you have questions, please ask." He grinned as he assessed the young women hungrily. One hand rubbed his hard-on, which was visible through his pants and in full view of everyone, except they weren't paying him any attention. But I was. I glared at him, hoping he could feel my gaze. He turned in my direction, licking his lips. "Did you come on your own, or are you with them?" he thumbed at the girls.

"I came on my own." I glanced at the others, then back at the mountain ranger with a raised eyebrow.

"Right, let's go." He moved through the sea of young, hot bodies until he was in front.

The women followed him while I brought up the rear. We traversed the beaten path up the mountain, dry grass and branches hitting our bodies.

The view was breathtaking as the mountain left a dark silhouette against the sky. It felt ominous as we followed the trail with our torches lighting the way. The girls in front giggled and flirted with Timothy. The one right in front seemed to like him the most as she kept touching his arm when she spoke. I rolled my eyes.

My lungs burned as we hiked, and my muscles pulled; but not as much as they should have. I was grateful to have started gym when I did, but I was used to indoor exercise, and outdoor exercise was different; the air, level of activity and atmosphere.

Each time we walked past a plant, insect, or tiny animal, Timothy gave us an explanation of what it was, where it originated from, what they ate and what they did out in nature. It was very educational, and I learned things I'd never heard before, but the other women were uninterested. All they did was giggle and fix their outfits. But Timothy knew I was listening as he kept glancing in my direction when he spoke. I suspected he knew I was mature compared to the others, and I appreciated a man who knew the difference between a woman and girls.

Timothy seemed around thirty-two. It was only a couple of years younger than me, yet he looked older. His skin was sun-kissed, and the fine lines around his eyes and mouth were prominent. He wore khaki clothing and a hat to match, but doubted it offered much protection from the sun. His green-coloured eyes held dirty secrets I couldn't imagine and felt his lust-filled gaze every so often caress my chest. He was definitely a breast man. The women were blessed in that department and flaunted it too much; leaving nothing to the imagination, therefore, leaving nothing wanting.

When we reached that first checkpoint, Timothy stretched his long, lean body where we could see him; along with the hard-on straining against the front of his pants. The girl who kept touching him approached him seductively as she stood closer. He smiled a toothy grin and sat on the bench. The other girls sat with their friends and watched the sun rise while I sat on the bench behind them.

Timothy glanced over his shoulder. "Come sit here; there's lots of room beside me." He scooted over, making space. I shrugged, stood up and sat beside him. He stretched his body back over the bench, lifting his arms above his head, then rested a hand on my shoulder and, I assumed, also on the girl's shoulder on his other side. Even though it was an eighties move he just pulled, I leaned into his side and caught the smell of him; aftershave with a hint of sweat. Strangely enough, his scent attracted me. His body was warm against mine even though I wasn't cold, and something about his demeanor was irresistible and charming. His personality was open to all as he welcomed everyone and made us all feel special, even though he had to share his time with us. Together, in comfortable silence, we watched the golden and pink sun rays splash across the sky and on the ocean as they did every day.

"You smell delicious," Timothy said near my ear, his breath hot against my neck, and goosebumps spread across my arms and down my back.

"It's something only fine women wear." I smiled seductively as I eyed the younger girl sitting beside him. He glanced at her, then back at me. He stared at me as if it was the first time he had truly seen me. The other girl was laughing and chatting with her friends, paying Timothy no attention.

"You are a fine woman." He stared hungrily, licking his lips.

We sat quietly for a few moments and stared at the wondrous sky and all that nature offered. The girls were chatty and didn't seem to pay any attention to their surroundings, and I wondered why they bothered to come on the hike if they weren't interested in it.

I closed my eyes for a moment and breathed in the mountain air with a hint of the ocean. The wind caressed my face and neck, making me shiver. I gave in to the elements surrounding me and listened to the waves crashing against the shore in the distance.

I flinched, opening my eyes, surrounded by a bloody mess.

Chapter Twelve

Blood covered the front of my body. My hands were inside her abdomen holding onto her soft organs. The other girls were beside her, their faces at peace, their bodies torn inside out.

Glancing up, I had bound Timothy to a tree with his arms tied above his head with a branch sticking out of his abdomen. He was being kept upright by his hands and that branch.

I gagged and swallowed hard.

The warm ichor of the girl I was straddling was sticky between my fingertips. My chest rose and fell as I processed my surroundings and shook my head.

How did this happen?

Why the women?

The women had done nothing to me. Surely it was only Timothy I was after. He was a sex-crazed mountain ranger who wanted nothing more than to fuck every single one of these girls.

Why would I want to hurt the young women?

Unless?

Unless...

They were hungry for what he offered because they were just like him. Every single one of them wanted more of the flesh; they were greedy and undeserving.

Exhaling slowly, I closed my eyes. I had to remember what had just happened.

What did I do?

Flashes came to mind. Timothy and I were sitting next to each other, and then he reached over, cupped my face and kissed me. His soft lips were on mine, his tongue begging me to open my mouth. He wanted to explore the depths of my very soul. As my lips parted, his tongue darted inside my mouth hungrily; moaning with each stroke of his tongue against mine. He grabbed my hand and pressed it against his throbbing cock, and together we stroked it over his clothing. He grunted with delight as our kiss intensified. All I thought about was him and what I wanted to do with his body in mine.

Then the girl beside him whined and complained she wasn't getting any attention. She pulled him away from me and kissed him. Then her friends circled us and began kissing him, each other, and then me. We stripped naked and touched one another. Our hot bodies rubbed skin to skin as flesh heated and as fingers caressed delicate folds and moist walls.

We were about to ignite a fire deep within ourselves.

The orgasm caught me off guard as the brunette's magical fingers worked my pussy; stroking the sensitive skin, pulling back the slippery hood and pushing her fingers into my wet channel. While her tongue pierced my mouth, playing sensual games with my tongue. She guided my hand to her clit so I could pleasure her as expertly as she satisfied me. She swallowed my screams as her mouth covered mine when we reached that peak of passion at the same time. We lay in each other's arms as our bodies dripped in a blissful sweat. She kissed me chastely, leaving me to go to her friend; leaving me alone and cold.

I shuddered at the abandonment.

I feared the loss of her.

The feelings didn't last long.

Timothy made his way to me, pushing my legs apart as he continued stroking his cock; getting ready to enter. He didn't wait for my consent as he slowly eased himself inside. Closing his eyes, he visibly relaxed in my embrace. He found his rhythm and started moving faster and deeper, building tension within my molten core until my body trembled uncontrollably.

A girl came in behind him. I wasn't sure what she did, but when she did it, Timothy stiffened and started pounding into me without restraint; building that sweet pressure within me, until I was ready to explode. My body tensed before the first hot wave washed over me and our orgasms hit us at the same time. I writhed beneath him when I felt his heat explode deep within me after one last thrust.

When he finished, he grunted in satisfaction and climbed off me. He gave me a lascivious wink and pulled up his pants without cleaning himself off. He rubbed his cock over his clothing as if that was good enough for him. My red panties were hanging around my right ankle, which I pulled up once I had wiped myself clean.

The young women were still naked and lying on their clothing next to each other and stared up at the sky while they spoke and laughed.

Today was my first sexual encounter with a woman, and

it was an experience to remember. The brunette glanced at me, smiling. She stood and sauntered in my direction.

"You were wonderful, Jasmine," she said, bending down, her large breasts hanging freely. She cupped my face in her soft, delicate hands and kissed me chastely. "If you want more of my sugar, here's my number." She handed me her business card; she owned a bakery. I tucked the card into my bag.

The sexually charged brunette walked towards a lustful Timothy, swaying her hips seductively from side to side. She wrapped her arms around his neck and kissed him like she was about to eat him. It was the same way she had kissed me, and I couldn't help but feel jealous.

I didn't appreciate her giving me the business card only to turn her back on me and kiss Timothy. We had shared a connection, but now... now it felt like she was trying to make me jealous; and I was jealous.

The other women were too busy to notice me. While Timothy and the brunette kissed, I stealthily approached and slit her throat from behind. She gasped, clutched at her neck and before Timothy could say anything, I did the same to him. Both collapsed to their knees, trying in vain to stop the bleeding.

Next, I approached the laughing women. One by one, I slashed their necks, too. A blonde woman jumped up and attacked me first. I grabbed her wavy hair, and we crashed hard to the ground with me straddling her waist and stabbing repeatedly.

Timothy climbed to his feet, and on shaky legs ran away with one hand holding his neck. I caught up to him and jumped, riding his body to the ground.

I pulled him to his feet, pulled the rope from his pocket,

and used it to tie him to a tree. As I pushed him against the tree, a branch impaled him.

A twig snapped behind me, and I spun around. The brunette was crawling away. I ran after her, jumped onto her back and straddled her. To stop her from squirming, I stabbed her over and over. She flipped onto her back and tried to take the knife from me, but I just kept stabbing, until finally she stopped moving, and my hands were inside her.

I was sick to the bone, but elated they were dead.

Every single one of them gone.

Chapter Thirteen

Dear Diary,

I don't understand how I blanked out today. It's never happened before. But after thinking about it and what was different this time around, I suspect it was the women and their behaviour. They were young and lustful, almost as much as Timothy was. Their mannerisms screamed at me, and I had to quiet them. Their sultry cries pulled on something so dark and deep within me I couldn't contain myself.

I had to soften their cries.

It was only after I had awakened and could breathe again that I realized what I'd done. It's not like me to behave that way.

Today was a mess!

I was dripping in their blood and searched for water, coming across a small spring to clean my body. The amount of wipes I had wouldn't have been enough to clean my body of their gore and filth.

That man didn't deserve more women. Timothy had had enough women to last him five lifetimes.

And those girls… they deserved worse.

What I did to them was a blessing; I had purged them of their sins.

It was only when their cries became silent that I calmed.

When I finally got home, which was only an hour ago, I scrubbed my body raw in the hottest shower I have ever had. I'm on my third glass of wine; a bottle I stole from the cellar. The rich oak flavour reminded me of Scott.

Also, I haven't eaten all day. I wanted to go to the coffee shop this morning after my hike, but with everything that had happened on the mountain, I couldn't stomach more human contact. Nor could I eat anything.

I needed it to be quiet.

I needed my thoughts to be still.

I needed to just be.

Now that I'm home, where it's safe, I can relax. There is nothing better than coming home where I can be myself. Where I don't have to pretend to be anything but me.

Although I heard those scratching noises again, I refused to investigate.

All I want is to relax on my balcony, read a magazine, and have a glass or four.

While I paged through the magazine, I noted an article about an artist who created the structures at the wine estate; Brandon.

And I can't explain it, but there is something about him that pulls me in…

Part VI

Chapter Fourteen

Dear Diary,

I don't know how many days have passed since the mountain episode, but visions of what had happened still flood my dreams. The blood and gore from those wenches cause me to wake up in cold sweats, leaving me wrapped in the damp sheets.

Last night was no different.

After another nightmare, I sat on my balcony chair to take my mind off the dream. Visions of their dead eyes flashed before me; one after the other. Then, something caught my eye and noted the walls in my bedroom had changed. On one side, the white walls were now a cream colour, while on the other side there were watermarks; which was strange since I recently had the house painted white and we have had no rain.

I don't understand what's happening.

A pain erupted in my chest as I steadied my breathing. My clothing clung to my body, and only after a long time of gazing upon the dark sea waters did I calm down.

While the crashing waves kept me captivated, the sounds from the house continued…

Once dressed, I collected the newspaper from my front door steps. Not wanting to go near crowds so early in the morning, I ate breakfast at home; yoghurt with muesli. As I paged through the newspaper, I noted an invitation to the opening of an art gallery on Main Street. It would showcase the same artist's work I'd seen at the winery.

Brandon's hair framed a delicate, yet manly, face. His soul-piercing brown eyes enthralled me as he stared at me from the ad. There was something alluring and familiar about the dark force that tugged at my soul. It felt like I had known him for years.

I turned the page and continued reading about the small town I now called home; the various sporting events, night hikes, and the sales on offer. I paged back to the advert and traced the artwork surrounding the words with my index finger. Perhaps I should attend. I didn't have plans, and I had a red dress I could wear. I would like to meet Brandon so that he could tell me more about his art. He created not only musical structures but also painted portraits.

They scheduled the event to start mid-afternoon, leaving me with a few free hours to do as I pleased.

I finished eating breakfast and walked the stone path towards the beach. It was a late Friday morning, so there were many people swimming already. I walked into the water until it reached my ankles. It was cool at first, but the longer I stayed there, the warmer it became.

When I passed the surf school, I couldn't remember seeing an article in the newspaper mentioning Scott, Codhi or Neville. Perhaps they were still investigating their deaths.

I was confident the newspapers would write something soon, and until then I would remain vigilant.

On the beach near the surf school, two teachers were showing six adults how to stand on their boards, then lie flat, then jump up again. There was a lot of laughter coming from the six adults, making me smile with them.

I walked past the surfers, vendors renting out umbrellas and chairs, and people suntanning. I ambled along the shore until I reached the pier and then turned around. It was a pleasant, windless, warm day, so I could spend some time at the beach.

Once I was back home, I changed into my red bikini, grabbed my beach bag, money, and my electronic reader. I followed the same route I had taken earlier and rented a chair.

I rubbed sunscreen over my body and sat down. Leaning against the chair back, I pulled out my electronic reader and continued with the new story I had started.

When the heat beat against my skin, leaving me sweaty, I enjoyed a dip in the sea. The water was cool against my hot flesh as I dived under the waves, tasting the ocean on my lips.

The surfers were still with the adult group, and their bouts of laughter made me turn to see what they were doing when a man tried to stand straight on his surfboard but kept toppling over. I smiled.

I frolicked in the water, and when I'd had enough of the salt; I went back to my chair, squeezing water out of my hair. A man sitting a short distance away from me waved. I flinched when he stood and walked towards me. I relaxed when I realized it was the man from the coffee shop.

"Jasmine," he said, wrapping his arms around me in a hug.

"Chris," I said, standing back, "who is manning the coffee shop while you're playing hooky?" I smiled mischievously.

"I'm taking a *'me day'*," he said using air quotes, "but I was there this morning to open. Where have you been?" he asked. "You haven't stopped by this. Is everything okay?"

"Everything is fine," I said, lying, hoping he couldn't hear the deception in my voice. "Today's my beach day, too."

"It's a beautiful day," he said, glancing around and then up at the sky.

"It is." I stepped closer to my things and grabbed my towel, wrapping it around my body.

"Anyway, let me leave you to your book. My turn for a dip."

"Enjoy, just mind the rip current to your left."

"Will do," he said, waving over his shoulder as he entered the sea.

I was sure he knew about the rip current since he'd lived here longer than I have, but I still wanted to warn him. There were natural dangers out there that could harm.

I sat in my chair and wiped most of the seawater from my body. My skin felt taut and sticky. My stomach grumbled; I was ready for lunch.

I handed my rental chair back to the vendor, returned to my spot to pick up my belongings, then looked out at the ocean. I searched for Chris and spotted him diving under a wave. The moment I started walking, he flailed his arms in greeting, and I waved back.

Laughing all the way home at Chris's ridiculousness, and how his bright blue eyes kept me from looking away. He was a homely person and seemed well-rounded and pleasant to be around. Perhaps if things moved along, he could be the *one*?

When I got home, I ate something small before I readied myself for the art gallery event. I showered, dried, pulled on red underwear and then my favourite red dress. The delicate fabric of the underwear complemented the soft lace of the dress, and once I added black heels, I was feeling much better than I did this morning.

Since the gallery was near my home, I walked there. Cars lined the narrow street as the crowd gathered near the gallery entrance. I approached the crowd as someone opened the doors.

The crowd pushed and bumped, forcing me to step backward to avoid getting hit when a man rushed past me, knocking me over. I crashed to the pavement, landing on my hands and knees. He stopped to help me up, apologizing profusely and swearing in-between. He helped dust sand off my knees, and when I stood straight, our eyes met. Those soul-piercing brown eyes captured me like they did this morning in the newspaper. My mouth parted and my eyes widened.

"Are you okay?" he asked again, holding my elbow. He dusted my dress and lightly hit my thigh.

"I'm fine, just stop hitting me," I said, smiling, and grabbing his hand, then calmly letting go. "I'm all right. You were in a hurry. Go on, you have an art exhibition to open." I nodded toward the entrance.

"How did you know?"

"I'm here to see your show." I smiled sweetly. "I'm a fan."

"And you are?"

"Jasmine."

"You have great cheekbones."

"Oh?"

"What I mean to say is, I would love to paint your portrait."

My cheeks heated. "You would?" I nervously touched my face.

"Absolutely, you're exquisite," he said. His dark gaze swept over my body, sending tingles up my spine. I shuddered at the thought of sitting naked as he painted me. "Are you available tonight?"

I arched an eyebrow.

"If you aren't doing anything after the show, allow me to paint your portrait."

It would be a wonderful experience. "I don't have plans, so yes," I said, smiling, "I'd love for you to paint my portrait."

"Good, it's a date," he said with a smirk. "Come, people await." He held out his elbow for me to take, which I did, and accompanied him inside.

Once we were inside, I was in awe of the various artwork he had created. From the statues carved from marble to the musical instruments he created. Hanging on the walls were detailed portraits of people; all shapes and sizes, some abstract; others with multiple colours swirling into each other as he blended deep purples with lilac. Each painting was unique.

"Look around, mingle, and have something to eat," he said near the shell of my ear. "I have a lot to do. Then later I'll find you. Please don't leave until I've painted you," he said with pleading eyes.

"I'll wait patiently," I whispered. "And I look forward to it." He took my hand in his and kissed my knuckles. "Whoever said chivalry was dead should be shot."

He chuckled devilishly, let go of my hand, and tended to his guests.

I grabbed a glass of champagne on offer by the server walking around and surveyed the landscape of pictures. With some of them, I felt nothing, whereas others tugged at my heart and soul. The emotional connection enveloped me as I stared at a woman lying down with red lace panties hanging loosely over her hips. It took me back to a time and place where I used to watch my mother embrace one of her many lovers. They had showered her with expensive gifts and ensured they took care of me too.

The woman in the painting seemed sad, her doe eyes staring straight past me; at someone behind me. Her glare also held questions nobody would answer. And it seemed the red lace was about to fall to the ground, or she was waiting for the man behind the paintbrush to approach her and tear the lace from her body, then capture her mouth with his.

Without thinking, my fingers touched my lips as if he'd kissed me. I heard him speaking to clients behind me, and as I turned; I met his gaze, and he smiled. He was sinfully beautiful and blessed multiple times. Though there had to be something wrong. No one was that perfect, yet he was.

As he moved across the floor, dark shadows played on his high cheekbones, his eyes finding mine. I walked to another portrait and out of his line of sight. When I looked again, he was gone, but I heard him speak with someone on the other side of the wall.

I walked around the floating wall to see what was on the other side, but by then he was gone. Glancing over my shoulder, and he was staring at me. I smiled. He smiled. He knew I had been watching him. But this was his game, and I was the mouse.

Chapter Fifteen

After about two hours, the crowd started thinning, leaving behind a handful of clients eager to buy art. The cleaning staff entered the room with their black bags and mops.

I stood in a corner with my eyes glued to the painting of the woman in red lace. I traced the lace near my collar, the soft fabric between my fingers.

"Beautiful, isn't she?" Brandon whispered into the nape of my neck. I shuddered, and a *gah* sound escaped my lips. "Did I frighten you?" he chuckled huskily.

I turned to look into his chocolate-brown eyes and smiled seductively. "Who is she?"

He glanced up at the painting. "Someone I once knew, but she passed away last year."

"I'm sorry."

"Don't be, we were only friends," he smiled sadly.

"If you're not up to painting my portrait tonight, you don't have to."

"You aren't getting out of it so easily," he said. "I'm still painting you today." He stared hungrily, but it wasn't food he was after. "I want to capture your beauty, Jasmine." He played with a loose strand of my hair. "We can go now if you like?" I glanced around and nodded. He grabbed my hand, leading me outside. "Let's do it now."

The sun had started setting, soft rays of gold and pink splashed across the sky as we walked across the road to the apartment buildings.

I giggled into my hand. "You live across the road?"

"Yes, what's so funny about that?"

"Yet you were still late for your own opening."

He chuckled lightheartedly. "Yeah, that is funny." We climbed the stairs to the first floor, stopping outside the only door. "My apartment comprises this entire floor." He shrugged nonchalantly. "My parents own the entire block, and not just the apartments."

"Wow, okay, who stays below or above you?"

"Whenever they visit, my sister stays above and my parents are below," he said, rolling his eyes. "I know what you're thinking, that I'm spoiled, right? My parents come from old money, and they like to look after their two children. I'm the only one who lives here, though, and they only visit once a year. My sister lives in the UK, and my folks are in the US."

"Why did you choose a small town off the coast of South Africa to be your home?" I asked.

"When we were young, we traveled to many countries, and South Africa is one I fell in love with. There are mountains to climb, oceans to swim in, forests to explore, hiking trails, beaches, and last but not least, the women are stunning." He pecked my cheek with soft lips. My cheeks heated as my loins tightened in anticipation. "Yes, the women here are magnificent, and there is much for me to do here." He regarded me with an intense stare, weighted with unspoken words.

He reached for my hand and showed me around his lavish apartment, every item costing millions; from the artwork of other famous painters to the structures from around the world. He was a collector of many things.

After he showed me his collection, we stopped outside a dark blue door. He unlocked it with a scan of his thumb. "This is where I keep the really expensive items," he said, opening the door and flicking on the light switch to reveal artifacts I'd only read about.

"Wow! How did you come by such exquisite items?"

"Bought from individuals or at auctions." He shrugged nonchalantly and walked to the Greywacke Statue Tribute to Isis. "I bought this from a man in Egypt. This was from an auction," he pointed at a silver cistern. They'd beautifully crafted the large item. "Philip Rollo designed and chiseled it. I was very lucky to get it."

"Everything is beautiful," I said as we walked along the wall. I saw a sword that belonged to Napoleon Bonaparte, jewelry, crowns, and even the Pinner Qing Dynasty Vase. "All this is worth billions."

"I'm not done though; there's still so much I want to acquire."

"When will it be enough?" I asked, wanting to touch the Vase but pulled my hand back in case the sweat from my finger shattered it.

He raised one shoulder. "I don't know. Maybe when I'm dead." He grabbed my hand. "Come, it's time to paint your portrait."

I followed him out of his walk-in safe, and he locked the blue metal door. We entered the open-plan art room, where a couch sat in the middle with blankets scattered everywhere.

"Lie over there," he pointed at the couch, "and if you feel comfortable enough to remove your dress, I would appreciate it. I want to capture all of your beauty, not have it hidden under clothing." He turned and started getting his paintbrushes and paints together.

I didn't feel he was a threat to me, so I removed my dress and underwear and sat on the couch.

When Brandon turned around, he froze, his dark stare raking up my body. "I love it when a woman owns her sexuality, and you are one exquisite specimen, Jasmine. If I could, I think I would keep you in my safe forever."

I frowned. I was not a piece of art he could collect and keep locked away. "Paint before the night gets old," I said, sounding grumpy.

He finished setting up and started painting. With each brush stroke across his canvas, it sent goosebumps all over my naked body. He painted, grunted, and adjusted his cock; no doubt straining against his tight pants. He permitted me restroom breaks, brought me a glass of wine so I could continue my relaxed pose. Then finally, after many hours and a stiff body, he turned the canvas for me to see.

He painted the soft lines of my body and the couch I was lying on. The detail of my face was striking considering he'd only painted for a couple of hours; it was stunning… an absolute masterpiece.

"I'm not done yet," he said with a smirk. "It isn't as wonderful as the original, but this is good for now. I'll continue working on it over the next week, since I've burned your face and body into my brain. I'll never forget you, Jasmine."

Brandon closed the gap, bent down and kissed me chastely. I wrapped my arms around his neck and opened my mouth. He dropped his paintbrush to the floor and pulled me against him. I moaned in his kiss, which only caused him to grunt in frustration as he tried to remove his clothing. Eventually, he ripped the buttons off his shirt and threw it to the ground. Then he kicked off his shoes, pulled off his pants, followed by his underwear; all while kissing me.

I smiled during his kiss as my hands roamed over the fine lines and definition of his toned body. I brushed lightly against the hairs on his chest, down his back, then grabbed his taut bum.

"Come with me." He walked me to the bed and threw me gently onto it. He had that look in his eyes, one that screamed *mine*.

As I lay on his bed, I opened my legs wide, inviting him.

He shook his head slowly. "So naughty, but I like it." He climbed onto the bed and hovered above me. "You ready for the best night of your life." I rolled my eyes and giggled when he pushed himself against my opening. "For that, I won't hold back."

"No, don't hold back. I want all of it, and I want all of you," I said lustfully, pulling him down to kiss me. I gave in to his deepening kisses as he pushed himself inside my flames of desire. The heat between us rose as he started hammering into me. He wasn't large, but he knew how to use his cock as he kept rubbing it skillfully against my G-spot and building that delicious combination of sensations between my legs.

Brandon grabbed my ass firmly with one hand as he pushed into me; his pounding savage-like. I moaned against his ear, which fueled his desires, making him sweat and groan as he pumped into me.

He was uncontrollable, and I couldn't stop the first orgasm hitting, knocking out my breath. I wrapped my legs around his waist, forcing him deeper. He grunted with animal-like fervor as he pushed his hips into me and orgasmed. I spasmed around him again, milking him, and he slowed his movements as his heat poured inside me. With one final push, he collapsed on top of me, out of breath. A cascading wave of tremors, contractions and aftershocks slammed into me. A layer of sweat covered our bodies as we melded into one.

"Yes, I definitely want to keep you," he said greedily. "I never want you to leave. Ever."

I was not an artifact, and I wasn't for keeps. He had no right to think I was someone to possess and do with as he pleased. Brandon was greedy, buying all those priceless items, and now he wanted me, too. As much as it hurt me to think this. As much as I adored his body and our lovemaking. He had to be punished.

My bag was on the bed near my head. I reached inside and grabbed the handle. As he lifted himself up to see what I was doing. I swept my blade down, severing his jugular. Blood rained down on me and inside my mouth; the sweet metallic taste as I swallowed him.

Brandon stood, grabbing his neck as blood sprayed everywhere; on his bed, floor and me. His eyes rolled into his head, and he collapsed to the floor.

Wiping my blade on his bedding, I tucked the knife back into my bag and went into his bathroom. His shower was large enough for an orgy of people, and his soaps were expensive. I washed my hair and lathered up with the

French liquid soap. When I was clean, I dried off with one of his white Egyptian towels.

Once dressed, I wiped down any item I thought I'd touched, grabbed my portrait, and exited his apartment. No one saw me leave his building, and I hurried home.

Chapter Sixteen

Dear Diary,

I really thought Brandon was the one. We had such a strong connection, but then he became possessive and wanted to acquire me like one of his items in his safe.

He was greedy in everything he did; from buying items to women to paintings. He wanted too much, yet he already had everything he needed.

Greed has no place in my heart.

Once I got home, I enjoyed a glass of wine; I may have had too much too quickly. It didn't bother me because the tension between my shoulder blades eased and I could relax.

I should've eaten something before having the wine, but I wasn't hungry. I drank my tablets with the last of my wine, relaxing me further.

I sat on my balcony chair and watched the delicate half-moon smile down at me.

I was at ease whenever I was home; it was my safe space away from everyone else. A place where I could be myself with no judgment.

I heard bouts of laughter again, but there was no-one outside or near my house, yet I heard the laughter as if they were in the next room.

I called out, but no-one answered.

Part VII

Chapter Seventeen

Dear Diary,

I awoke early again. The sleepless nights are taking their toll on my body and possibly my mind; I'm exhausted yet I can't sleep.

The tablets I take don't help, and I suspect I may have to change them again.

The noises from within the house are no longer as disturbing as they once were, or I'm getting used to them.

The third floor continues calling out to me. Again this morning I stood at the top of the stairs and stared down the dark hallway.

I don't recall ascending the steps to the third floor, but I was there. It was as if I were waiting for something to happen, but nothing did. I laughed at my silly thoughts. Yet I wasn't foolish enough to continue down that dark hallway.

I ate breakfast at that little coffee shop. Brought my diary with me so I could continue jotting down my thoughts while I ate.

Christopher greeted me and asked me out on a date, which I'm considering…

"I'll even cook," he said with a wink. "Something as special as you."

I stared into his bright-brown eyes as I contemplated the invitation. I had nothing else on this evening, and he seemed nice enough. We'd meet up for dinner and get to know each other better.

"That sounds fine. What time should I come around?" His coffee shop was only open for breakfast and lunch, then closed around three in the afternoon.

"I'll keep one or two staff on so they can serve us, but come around five." Someone was calling him, but he waited for me to respond before he tended to their complaint.

"Sure," I said, nodding. "I'll see you here at five."

"Excellent, I look forward to it. Any special requirements? Any allergies?"

"No allergies, and I eat everything."

He nodded once, knocked on the table, and apologized for leaving. He approached the old woman with a smile, and whatever he said to her, made her smile, too.

I continued eating my breakfast and read the newspaper that was freely available. An old man sat at a table to my left, and he kept staring. It looked like he wanted to say something, but then he pursed his lips and continued with his meal. I wasn't sure if he recognized me or had seen me during my activities this week, but I couldn't eat. *Did he see me? Did he know what I'd done?*

The old man paid and when he stood up to leave, he stopped at my table before passing. "Sorry, miss, but you look so much like my niece, Margaret. What is your name?"

Oh, thank goodness it was just that, and the tension between my shoulders eased. "My name is Jasmine."

"Jasmine," he said, repeating my name as he shook his

head, "you look so much like my niece. She would've been about your age now."

"What happened to her?"

"I don't know." He shrugged. "My sister wasn't quite all there, if you know what I mean." He swirled a finger near his head, emphasizing she was crazy. "And she would tell me stories about her daughter and how sick she was. Then, one day, they both disappeared. I listed them as missing at the police station, but they never found them. They vanished. Someone ransacked my sister's big house, and their clothing was missing. So, either they ran away or someone made it seem that way. Anyway, you just look like what my niece might have looked like if she were here now. Sorry to have disturbed you."

I had nothing to say to the old man, and didn't trust my voice. The back of my throat hurt when I swallowed. I watched him put his hat on and exit the coffee shop. I threw money on the table, packed my belongings and followed him.

The old man walked towards the beach but didn't go to the beach. He continued along the walkway until he came upon a block of apartments and entered it. I stood on the pavement staring up at the building and noted that I'd never walked this side of town before. Apartment buildings stretched along the beachfront, where owners either came for holidays or rented out their apartments to holiday goers.

Since I didn't have access to the building and didn't want to frighten the old man by following him inside, I continued walking along the beachfront.

The story he told reminded me of my own; a young mother and her daughter having to disappear late one evening. Never to be seen again. Until we arrived in Joburg.

"Did you remember something?" I flinched at his voice.

The old man stepped closer with a smile stretching across his face. "Do you remember me?"

I shook my head as he towered over me. Walking backwards, I tripped over a step and fell to the ground. I stretched my arms out to stop the fall but landed on my bum, hurting my palms. "Ow," I cried, rubbing gently on my hands to ease the burn.

"Let me help you up," the old man said, reaching for my hand, but I waved him away. "My name is Keith. When I noticed you following me, I knew I had to fetch the photo I still had of you." He showed me a picture of a little girl with pig-tails, chubby cheeks, and the worst clothing imaginable on a six-year-old in the eighties. The little girl wore brown corduroy pants and a dirty lime green satin shirt. Cringe worthy.

I took the picture and studied it. "Even though we look eerily similar, this is not me." I handed back his photo. "Sorry. Even our stories are similar, but we aren't family." I stood and dusted my hands on my pants. They stung from the sweat, sand, and the friction from my pants. I needed to wash them. To my left was a couple of outdoor showers people used after their swim in the sea. I walked over and rinsed my hands.

The old man's face drooped with disappointment. "It's a pity," he said sadly. "It would have been nice to have family around." He pursed his lips and blinked away tears.

"Keith," I said. "We might not be family, but we could be friends, if you like?" I dried my hands on my shirt. "I'm new in town and could use a friend." My smile reached my eyes.

He chuckled. "My dear, why would you want me to be my friend? I imagine you can make friends easily." He eyed me from head to toe, then raised an eyebrow. "No husband or boyfriend?"

"Not yet," I said, grinning. "I'm looking for the perfect one."

He laughed louder. "I hate to break it to you, but there is no such thing. The closest you will ever get to *perfect* is to live with your lover, boyfriend, or husband without wanting to kill him."

I laughed, but it sounded hollow and forced even to me. Little did he know I was determined to find *my* version of a perfect man, but I went along with his joke. "Well, there's nothing wrong with dating a few men to find someone who fits my version of perfect."

"No, definitely not," he chuckled, and his entire body shook. He pocketed the picture and then added. "Like my neighbour always says, *'Why buy the pig? When you can have the bacon for free'*." He roared with laughter. It was funny, and I laughed along.

"Thanks, Keith, I needed some laughter today." I started walking back the way I had come. "I have to go, but I'll see you around. Perhaps at the coffee shop for breakfast sometime?"

"That would be lovely," he said. "I'm there every morning."

Chapter Eighteen

I had to get ready for my date, and the walk following Keith around left me sweaty. I opted to take a bath instead of my usual shower and sighed as I climbed into the hot water. Leaning backwards, I ensured the water covered me from neck to toes, soothing my aching muscles and joints.

Perhaps Chris was my Mr. Perfect. I smiled at the thought of having a partner who owned a coffee shop.

I reached for the glass of red wine and enjoyed a long sip. I picked up my electronic reader and found a light horror ebook filled with short stories I couldn't wait to sink my teeth into, chuckling at the thought.

I loved my bathroom. There was a freestanding bath with golden claws standing in the middle of it. Frosted glass and a frosted door surrounded the shower in the corner. Inside the shower were two jets that stood at an angle and pointed down at the person showering. If I switched both taps on, I enjoyed a water massage. But right now I wanted to relax in the bath.

I read a few pages of the horror story and was halfway

through my wine when that scratching sound started up again. It reminded me of nails digging into concrete and as tiny bits of concrete chipped away; the nail tore and the skin became raw. I shuddered at the thought. I set the book and wine on the floor and washed up.

Making a mental note for later; I wanted someone to check for mice or insects in the walls. For now, I would ignore the noise.

Feeling fresh and relaxed from my bath, I decided once I was ready I'd walk to the coffee shop; the day was too beautiful to waste driving in a car. The area was safe to walk alone at night because of the surveillance cameras and police presence. Since I was having a late lunch/early dinner, I chose a summer dress that was elegant yet informal.

As I left my bedroom, a creaking sound echoed from the third floor. Shaking my head, I wanted to know what that was but ignored it for now. The creaking sound neared as I approached the stairs from my bedroom. I didn't want to go up. When I took the first step down, the creaking sound boomed louder. A cold sweat dripped down my back.

Squeezing the banister until my fingers ached, I slowly ascended the stairs leading to the third floor. Staring up at the ceiling, I noted a brown watermark had blossomed during my stay, and I couldn't remember it ever raining. I took the next step up, and the creaking softened. Then, with the next step up, the creaking seemed to have moved backwards.

Once I was on the third floor, I stood motionless. It was still light outside and there were no curtains in either of the rooms, yet it was dark as shadows played against the walls. I couldn't see where the wall ended, and the shadows began; it was like a bottomless hole at the end of the corridor.

Flinching at the sound of the reminder on my cellphone, I hurried down the stairs. The creaking followed me and was loud enough to make the windows vibrate. I opened the front door, slammed it shut, and everything became quiet.

My chest rose and fell as I sucked in sea air. I pressed my head against the front door, feeling the cold seep in. My arms pebbled, and sweat dripped down my face. I needed to shower again, but I'd be late if I did.

Shaking the feeling off that it was all in my mind, that there was nothing wrong with the house, it's only my imagination. I walked the steps down my private path towards the beach. The surfers were teaching a group of kids how to stand on their boards in the water; people were walking along the sand, with a few still suntanning. As if something was calling me, I turned back to look at my house. The paint had peeled off the walls; the windows needed cleaning, and my front door needed varnish. Frowning at the sight, I made another mental note to have the contractors come to the house again and do all those things *again*. I had already paid them to do this, yet my house still looked the same as when I'd first arrived.

The lines between my eyes deepened as I thought about the dates the contractors were here, but I couldn't remember. As I headed towards the coffee shop, I thumbed my cellphone on and went to my calendar to check; there was nothing written this last month showing the appointment. I pressed the plus sign to make a new reminder in my calendar to call the contractors tomorrow morning.

By the time I closed the application, I was standing outside the coffee shop. The sign read, *'Closed'*, but I saw Chris pointing a finger at one waitress. His face was red, and he was yelling at her. She covered her eyes as the tears flowed. When I knocked, she glanced up at me, turned and ran into the ladies' bathroom. Chris straightened his back when he saw me, plastered on a fake smile and approached.

"Jasmine, you're right on time. Please come in," he said, opening the door.

"Are you sure? It looks like I'm interrupting something?" I glanced at the ladies' bathroom door.

Chris turned to see what I was referring to. "Ah, that's nothing, just a little misunderstanding."

"It didn't look like nothing."

His eyes darkened as he leered down at me. "It doesn't concern you, Jasmine." His tone was harsh and dripped with malice.

What a shame!

I was looking forward to enjoying just dinner. Now I could look forward to my special dessert afterwards. I stared up at him and smiled sweetly. "I'm hungry. What are we eating tonight?"

His demeanor softened as his shoulders sagged, and he exhaled. His smile matched mine, and he pointed at a table in the corner. "You'll love it." I walked to the corner and placed my bag on the ground near the first seat and sat down.

"For starters, we have chicken soup with a dumpling," he continued.

My mouth watered at the thought, and I licked my lips. "Sounds divine."

"For dinner we have pork chops with mashed potatoes and corn, and for dessert I made crème brûlée."

I rubbed my stomach for added effect. "That sounds wonderful, Chris."

He spun around with enthusiasm and headed towards the bar. He returned carrying an ice bucket with a bottle inside. Blood dripped from one side of his face down his naked body. I sat straighter in the chair and blinked, and it was only him walking towards me. He sat the ice bucket between us, removed the bottle, and poured some bubbly liquid into my glass.

"French champagne for the beautiful lady," he said seductively, handing me the glass.

"*Merci*," I cooed and took the glass he offered. He poured some into his glass and returned the bottle to the ice bucket and sat down.

"I thought you might enjoy some fine dining in my little coffee shop," he said, clinking gently against my glass. I blinked, and blood and gore covered his face. The left side of his face was open, with parts of his brain exposed.

I swallowed hard as I stared at him, blinking a few times as I sipped on the champagne. When the bubbles hit my tongue, and I swallowed, Chris's face was normal again. The last time I had these types of visions, it was after they'd adjusted my dose. I downed the champagne and set the empty glass on the table. Glancing at my cellphone again, I thumbed to open it and checked the calendar again. I couldn't remember the last time I'd taken my medication.

Chris's mouth was moving, but all I heard was the blood in my ears and my heart thumping in my chest. When I blinked again, his face was gone, as if he'd shot his face off with a shotgun. All that remained was part of his jaw with a few teeth still embedded in the bone, his tongue hung loosely down to his chest, and the back of his skull and brains were visible. I pushed my chair back as I stood, knocking it over.

"Are you alright?" Chris reached for me.

The waitress he had reprimanded when I'd arrived came through the swinging doors with two bowls on a tray. I hadn't seen her come out of the bathroom and enter the kitchen. She stopped mid-step and stared at us with a shocked expression. "Should I come back?" she asked meekly.

"No, it's fine," I said, my voice shaky. "I'm fine. I think I'm just hungry." My smile wavered at the sides as I picked up the chair and sat down.

"Are you sure?" Chris asked. "We can do this another time if you're feeling unwell?"

"No, I'm fine. I want to try your soup." I smiled sincerely up at the poor girl. The bowls made a clanging noise from her non-stop shaking hands. She placed the bowls in front of us, and we started eating.

Once I ate a spoonful, I felt better. Chris wasn't morphing into a devil's nightmare, and I was enjoying myself again.

Chris was charming and funny, but every time the poor waitress entered to clear the dishes, or bring us the next meal, he made it clear he disapproved of her. It wasn't the way she placed the items in front of us; he despised *her* as a person.

After she offered dessert, Chris entered the kitchen to chastise her. His yelling intensified when she started crying. Apparently he thought the food was cold, the dessert not cold enough, or she did nothing the way he wanted. His temper tantrums were beyond the norm, and I felt sorry for the waitress.

I finished my crème brûlée and stood. Chris's behaviour towards the poor girl was uncalled for, and it had to stop.

"Go home!" I yelled, bursting through the swinging door and entering the kitchen. Chris had his hands on her shoulders, squeezing her. Pain flashed in her eyes, then relief when she saw me. "That's enough, Chris. Nobody should treat her that way." I pointed at her, then thumbed behind me. "Go."

The girl nodded and ran out.

Chris silently glared daggers at me. Hate radiated from him. "How dare you interrupt me while I'm busy with one of my staff?"

I lifted an index finger to shush him. When I heard the door close and the annoying bell chime, with my thumb I removed the strap of my dress from my shoulder.

"Oh!" he exclaimed and started unbuttoning his shirt. By the time my dress fell to the floor, Chris was naked, wearing only a naughty grin. "You are full of surprises, Jasmine."

"I like to keep it exciting."

With one hand I rubbed his cock, the other massaged his nipple. He stepped closer. I placed my hands on his chest and slowly caressed down his front. He gripped my shoulders, keeping me in place. Trailing below his belly-button, down the path of hair leading to his hard muscle; I gripped it in both hands. He moaned, tilting his head backwards as I stroked slowly and purposefully, building up pleasurable intensity before stopping. He glanced down, licked his lips, and pushed me towards a workbench that stood against the wall with various kitchen items on top.

"My turn," he said, removing my red lace panties. He crouched down, pushing my legs apart. I leaned against the workbench as his fingers and tongue found my sensitive, slick folds. He licked, sucked and fingered. I wrapped my legs around his shoulders as he kept my hips in place. As I held on to the table behind me, he continued piercing his tongue into me then stopped before I climaxed. Feeling cheated, I stared at him with a shocked expression. He chuckled naughtily. "Hop on," he said, tapping the workbench.

He helped me onto the bench, which was the right height; I scooted my backside close to the edge, which allowed him access to rub his cock up and down my slick pussy, readying me for his penetration by coating his shaft with my juices. He let out a low groan when he couldn't wait any longer and slid slowly inside. I pushed my hips into him, an invitation for him to go deeper, but he continued his slow tease; I trembled in anticipation. The paradox of sensations from his glare to his slow movements caused me to writhe in frustrating pleasure.

"Fuck me now," I groaned greedily.

He leaned forward, his hot breath against my neck. "I will make you scream," he said lustfully. He bit my shoulder playfully, gripped my hips with force, then started thrusting into me. His movements were slow at first, with purposeful strokes, until his rhythm became harder and faster. Each thrust hit my G-spot until the intensity became too much, and I squeezed his cock like a vice as the first orgasm hit me, but Chris didn't slow down. He continued his pounding until he stopped and dug his nails into my hips as he released his heat within me. My second orgasm caused me to spasm around him again, his cock twitching as I leaned back enjoying the pleasant contractions; wave after wave.

He lay on top of me on the workbench. When I tried to sit up, he moved off me. "Do you do this often, Chris?"

"Huh? What?"

"Sleep with women inside your kitchen. Your workbench is suspiciously the right height for you?"

He climbed off the workbench and started dressing. "It's happened a few times."

"And that waitress, was she one of them?"

"I don't do this kind of thing often, Jasmine. Will you tell me yours if I tell you mine?"

That was an affirmative answer without his having to say anything. No wonder the poor girl was upset; she was jealous. He made her feel worse by keeping her here all afternoon and yelling at her in front of me. He was a mean bastard.

Climbing off the workbench, I sauntered past him, picking up my dress and underwear. We continued dressing in silence then when I pulled my dress on; I saw the wall beside me.

I grabbed the butcher knife from the magnet on the wall and slashed down the front of him before he had time to react. Raising my hand high, I brought it down hard onto his skull, cracking it. His eyes bugged as he stared, his only reaction. I tried pulling the knife out of his head, but I'd lodged it deep inside. The magnet where I'd taken the butcher knife held four other knives. I grabbed the next biggest one and slashed his throat. It was only then that he crashed to his knees and fell backwards; his mouth parted, eyes bulging, and blood pooling.

"You should have been nicer, Chris." I crouched near his lifeless body. "Your food was delicious though." I sucked some dessert off my finger.

Chapter Nineteen

Dear Diary,

Tonight was delicious. I really enjoyed myself.

Chris would have been wonderful husband material, but after his wrath on that poor girl, I couldn't stand it anymore. I had to teach him a lesson; one that would cost him his life. He was a good fuck, but he was not a nice person.

Even though I'd told Keith I would go to the coffee shop for breakfast, I think I'll be avoiding it for a while. Especially since that waitress knew I was the last person to see Chris alive. I would have to wait and see. Perhaps the police would knock on my doorstep soon. There were too many unsolved murders; someone had to have seen something.

I needed to stop what I was doing, but these men did this to me. These men were cruel. They were deadly in their own wicked way, bringing the darkness out of me.

I was helping the women they hadn't met yet, and I was protecting them from these men.

Perhaps that's my calling, to eradicate the evil wrongdoers from this world.

Part VIII

Chapter Twenty

Dear Diary,

My phone stopped working, and I can't find my charger. I don't know what day it is. The sun continues to shine brightly outside, and the waves still crash onto the sand. The world continues around me even though I have no concept of time.

The creaking sounds reverberate within the house, and it feels as though it's in my bones.

The deep-seated echoes and darkness surround me.

Once I'd showered, I wanted to dress but found my closet empty and my laundry basket was full of dirty clothing. When I walked through the house in search of my washing machine, I couldn't find it even though I remembered the moving company had brought it in from their truck and they'd connected it for me.

I don't know what's going on anymore.

The third floor still calls, egging me on, pushing me towards the edge of the abyss; a place I don't want to go to.

I need my tablets.

I searched through the kitchen cupboards and all the bathrooms, but I can't find my medication. I can't remember the last time I drank any of it.

Someone is here…

The doorbell chimed again. Grabbing the cleanest dress out of the laundry basket, I pulled it on, and hurried down the stairs. I opened the door to a clean-cut young man holding a package. He stared with big blue eyes and a jaw almost on the floor.

"Can I help you?"

"Are you Miss Beukes?" he asked, glancing at the package to read the name, then back at me.

Nodding. "Yes, that's me," I said, opening the door for him to enter.

"Wow, your house is beautiful," he said, staring past me.

I stared in the direction he was looking at and frowned. Dirt lined the floors, the walls were turning yellow from water stains, and the cracks had enlarged since the last time I looked. The place was turning into a dump faster every day. I glanced at the portraits and was relieved they were still in great condition.

"And the artwork," the delivery guy said, placing the package on the table in the foyer, and walked up to the painting. "Is this an original?" he asked, touching it delicately.

I nodded. "Yes, everything I own is an original." I followed him into the living room. I had covered my furniture with plastic to keep the dust and water off since I hardly used it. The room smelled damp and mouldy, and an icy feeling washed over me. My chest rose and fell as I sucked in cold air and tried to steady my frantic heart. This was not how I remembered the room. When I exhaled, I saw my breath in front of me. I surveyed the room; it still held the expensive artwork, my furniture and the large mirrors on the walls, but the room itself was run down and weathered.

"Wow! Sorry, that seems to be the only thing that's coming out of my mouth, but your house is magnificent." He stood in the middle of the room and then faced me. "What's wrong?" he asked. "Did I say something to upset you?"

"Don't you see it?" I asked, panic laced in my tone.

"What?" he shrugged.

"The paint peeling off the walls?" I pointed to the wall nearest us. "The water stains on the ceiling and wall." He shook his head with a confused expression. "Can't you smell the dampness?"

"Ma'am," he said with concern. "I don't know what's going on, but your house is in perfect condition," he waved his hands in the air. "There is nothing out of place and no funky smells. Your mansion is lovely." He stepped closer. "I would kill to have a house like yours. You should see my place, now that is a dump." He grinned.

Anger flooded me, possessed me. My vision tunneled until all I saw was his head surrounded by darkness. My pulse thundered in my ears as pins and needles washed over my body.

I lunged at the young man and rode his body to the ground with my hands around his neck and my knees on his chest. He made strange choking sounds as I cut the air from his lungs. He gripped my arms and tried to pry my hands off him, but I squeezed his neck as hard as I could. His pulse thumped beneath my fingertips as I applied pressure, and his skin was hot to the touch. He tried to grab something to hit me with, but there wasn't anything he could use.

This kill was different; I had no knife, forcing me to use my hands. It was difficult, personal, and took time; not like the others that were quick and bloody.

As I sucked in air, the walls darkened and closed in on me. The cracks enlarged, and the abyss was about to swallow me.

I let go of his neck, fell off his body, and pushed myself against the wall. The dark void receded into the wall, and the watermarks stopped spreading. Glancing at the man I attacked, his arms fell limply to his sides and his bloody blue eyes were vacant. His neck was red and swollen.

Why did I do it? What came over me? Why hurt the man? But I did. He envied my house. Envied my things. He had to die.

I looked up and the house slowly decayed, weathered by the elements. The cracks were spreading, and the water damage was everywhere. A damp, earthy smell wafted through the surrounding air. It was then I realized my house was crumbling with me still inside.

I turned towards the young man lying motionless on my floor. He saw the house as it was. I couldn't understand how he saw it differently from me.

I shook my head, stood, and walked to the table.

The package.

I picked it up, shook it, but nothing moved inside. Grabbing a pair of scissors from the kitchen, I placed the package on the kitchen island and cut the sides. Once opened, I flipped the lid to see what was inside.

I froze, my blood running cold. I stepped backwards until I reached the kitchen cupboard. As I walked back to make sure what I saw was correct, the delivery guy ran into me, throwing me to the ground. He knocked the wind out of me, and as I gasped for air, he wrapped his fingers around my neck.

Spit dripped from his mouth. "You tried to kill me, bitch," he yelled. His glassy blue eyes glowed, framed by his petechiae eyes. "What the fuck is wrong with you, woman?" he growled low into my face as his fingers curled around my neck. He squeezed; he wanted to hurt me as much as I'd hurt him, but he couldn't. Luckily for me, he didn't have it in him to hurt me. He couldn't hurt me. He let go of me and sat back, still straddling my waist.

"I'm sorry," I whimpered. "I didn't mean to hurt you, but you scared me."

"Jeez, man, I don't know what you are going through, but you can't attack people like that," he said in a hoarse whisper; a side effect from me bruising his throat.

"I don't know what's going on with me. Sorry." I sounded hoarse myself, but not as bad.

A silent moment passed between us as we stared at each other. He gave his full attention, surveying me with open appreciation.

"My name is Colin." He climbed off me and pushed himself against the cupboard, leaning his head against it as he caught his breath.

I sat up, crossed my legs, and rubbed the tender skin near my larynx. A headache blossomed at the back of my head from hitting it against the kitchen floor.

"Sorry if I hurt you," he said, sounding sincere.

"Me too." My smile wavered. I regretted hurting him. It was wrong of me to do that to him. Even though he admired my things, envied them, it was me who saw things differently. It was always me. "Can you forgive me?"

"Well," he said, rubbing his neck. "That all depends on

what you do to make it up." A smile reached his twinkling blue eyes.

"How about," I said, thinking, "I make you dinner?" I glanced up at the wall to find I had no clocks anywhere.

Colin lifted his wrist and glanced at his watch. "Well, it is almost dinner time. I might as well eat something." He climbed to his feet, gripped the counter for balance, then leaned against it to stay upright. "So, where shall we start?"

He helped me stand, feeling disoriented myself, but held onto him while I regained my footing. My vision tunneled, and sparkly stars flooded the room. Blinking vigorously until I could see my surroundings again, I got to work making dinner.

There was a chicken in the freezer, which we placed into a pan and into the oven. While the chicken cooked, Colin helped chop vegetables to make a salad. He made me laugh when he opened a bottle of white wine, which we sipped on while preparing dinner. He loved to cook and showed me a few tricks with the knife.

After an hour everything was ready, and we sat at the kitchen table. We shared stories about where we came from, what we did for fun, and what our dreams were.

"I'm working this stupid job to pay for my studies and pay the rent, but it's not something I want to keep doing." He raised a shoulder. "I get tired going door to door delivering stuff for other people. Seeing all the nice things they already own makes me want to succeed even more." He stared at something as he spoke, as if he was dreaming of a new life far away from here. Perhaps he had hopes and dreams and was determined to realize them.

"With your determination, Colin, you will do great things," I said, patting his hand. "Just keep at it, but stop envying everyone around you. Focus on *your* dreams. Envy is a root cause of evil."

He nodded. "You're right. I need to make it my own." He smiled. It relieved me to see that the swelling around his neck had subsided, and his eyes were no longer red. "And thanks for dinner," he said, placing his knife and fork on his empty plate. "This was a pleasant turn of events."

"Well, you did most of the cooking."

"You helped," he said, staring. The hunger in his eyes was not for food. I exhaled sharply, and my cheeks flushed. His gaze intensified, making me uncomfortable and making me need to change the subject.

"How are you feeling?" I asked, cringing inwardly. The guilt.

"I'll be fine. How are you?" He glanced at my neck, then at my face.

"I'm good." I glanced around the room and found the walls were white, and the kitchen counter pristine. Everything was just as it was. Everything was back to normal. I smiled. "You know what? I think everything will be fine."

It was still early, and Colin wanted ice-cream to soothe his aching throat. Guilt-ridden, I suggested a walk to the ice-cream shop since I didn't have any in the freezer. We walked down my private path and onto the beach. When I looked over my shoulder, the fresh white paint was pristine, and the windows and doors were as good as new. I had only imagined it as a ruin. Relief washed over me; it was all in my head.

We walked along the beach, and as we came upon the surf clubhouse; I saw Codhi. I stopped dead, blinking and swallowed hard.

"Are you okay?" Colin asked, his voice sounding far away, but it brought me back into the now.

"Yes, I'm fine, thought I saw something." My voice sounded strained and unsure. I didn't believe what I was saying and doubted Colin did either; he didn't have to know me well to hear my lie.

Codhi was alive and well and teaching a group of young kids how to stand on their surfboards on the sand before trying it out on the water. My chest heaved. My hands were clammy; my clothing clung to my body. Yet, it was a comfort to know that Codhi was alive, and that what had happened between us was just in my head.

I couldn't understand it though; it had all felt real. His blood was warm on my hands, dripping between my fingers, as my knife sliced through his soft flesh. I shuddered at the thought and pushed the strange dark memory aside.

I would look at this realisation as something positive; I was not a cold-blooded killer as I had thought.

My heart swelled to see Codhi helping the kids. I wiped a tear away, knowing that I'd been gravely mistaken; that Codhi was not as lazy as I'd perceived him to be.

We continued walking until we reached the small coffee shop. Chris was inside chatting to the same waitress, and they both smiled. He wasn't the mean, angry guy I had thought he was, who yelled at his staff.

Then, Neville approached us on the pavement, and my heart started beating rapidly, and I had to remember to breathe. He passed us to go inside the coffee shop, looked up and our eyes met. He winked, which caused my heart to thump against my chest, and I was sure everyone heard the beat. I pressed my palms against my legs to steady the shaking. Neville was my gym partner, or so I'd thought. He had an arm draped over a woman who was laughing at his jokes. They entered the coffee shop and sat at a table.

Again, seeing these men alive and walking around only

highlighted the fact that perhaps I was delusional. That I'd imagined those gory deaths and what I'd done to them. What made it worse, I'd enjoyed killing them. I relished the fact that I'd hurt them so badly for things I'd made up in my mind. Those men weren't like I'd imagined them at all.

Nothing like this had ever happened to me before.

Why now? Why here?

As we approached the ice-cream shop, Scott had bought an ice-cream for his son and daughter. They thanked their dad and walked to their car. Scott was the manager at the winery, and I was ecstatic to know that he was a kind and caring father. As I watched them climb into their car and drive away, a Jeep drove by, and I recognized the mountain ranger. He had a young girl beside him, and they were singing to music.

Colin ordered us each an ice-cream; mine had a chocolate flake in it, and I had to lick quickly to avoid it dripping over my hand. We traversed towards the beachfront market, where an artist was taking down his portraits before nightfall. Brandon glanced at me, smiled, and continued packing them away. There was a portrait of a woman lying on a couch who looked eerily like me, but I brushed it off as a coincidence. I smiled as we passed him.

Colin and I sat in silence on the bench near the beach and ate our ice-creams. The comfortable seaside atmosphere put my mind at ease.

Everything had just been a figment of my crazy imagination. I killed no-one.

None of it was real.

They weren't the monsters I'd projected them to be.

Which relieved me because I wasn't the killing kind.

Chapter Twenty-One

I waved Colin goodbye and closed the door behind me, dead-bolting it. Colin and I had another date tomorrow, and I was excited to have another normal evening out. Even though he was younger by a few years, he was mature with an old soul.

The attack brought us together in a strange, twisted way. While the dinner we shared was my first authentic experience with the opposite sex in years. I connected with him on an emotional level, and the only intimacy we shared was when he kissed me goodnight; it was electric. A shiver ran through my body, a shudder of pleasure, as I thought of his kiss.

In that moment, I knew that being with Colin would be a slow process and that I would grow to love him. There would be no instant gratification.

Leaning against the front door with my head back and my eyes closed, I remembered the reason Colin had knocked on my door. *The package.* He'd asked what it was, but I said it was stuff I'd ordered. I couldn't tell him what was inside. He wouldn't understand. I didn't understand it myself.

The foyer was bright when I opened my eyes. The white walls surrounded me, and the portraits on the walls stared back, and the living room was still perfect. The lines between my eyes deepened. It was different earlier. The house was decaying, and now, after almost being choked to death, everything was as it should be.

Was it all back to normal, and would it stay that way now? I wasn't sure what normal was anymore, just as long as I didn't *kill* anyone.

Shaking my head, I pushed away from the door and entered the kitchen. The box sat on the counter and seemed to glow.

The kitchen was how I'd remembered it; everything in its place. No more sickly dripping paint or brown water stains. Even the washing machine and dishwasher were where I'd remembered them being.

Did I have to die before my reality shifted into perspective? I shuddered at the thought.

Perhaps I was the one slowly dying, and Colin had woken me up. Saving me from myself.

Opening the lid of the package, I cast my eye at the contents of the box. I pulled the note out first:

"Dear Margaret,

You left before you could pack your belongings, so I thought I would do it for you and ship them to your new address. I hope everything is as you dreamed.

Everybody misses you in the group, and they send their love.

We knew you could make it in the big bad world, and as much as we want you to visit us, don't.

Don't return!!

You need to look to your new future.
All our love,
'Jasmine'

I wiped stray tears from my cheeks and placed the note on the counter. All this time I was using Jasmine's name instead of my own. I'd created a new persona in a new town. A fantasy of anonymity.

The next item I removed from the box was a book I always read, *'The Seven Deadly Sins'*, my hairbrush, red underwear, a summer dress, four bottles of prescription medication, and my red velvet diary.

I glanced at the full medication bottles, realizing I'd taken none since arriving here. Perhaps that's why my memory had altered, making me feel like I was losing my mind.

A thought crossed my mind.

But why was I so afraid of the third floor? It was part of the puzzle I had to solve. *What had kept me from going into those rooms and what would happen if I went there now?*

I kept the book and diary in my hands and ascended the stairs to the third floor. The corridor was not as dark or gloomy as I'd imagined. Slowly, I approached the first bedroom; Mom's favorite bedding still covered her bed, her full-length mirror stood in the corner, her dressing table stood to one side, and on the other side stood her closet with her clothing. The blinds were open, and I welcomed the moon's kisses as it reached inside Mom's room and splashed onto me.

Turning towards the other bedroom, mine, it was just as I'd left it. As we had left it all those years ago. My teddies sat neatly on my bed, with my pink bedding and a purple pillow waiting for my return. My table and chair were on one side, with a trunk full of toys. Against the far wall was my closet full of clothing for a six-year-old.

The memories came flooding back.

My uncle had hurt me. Mom didn't hesitate. She packed us up, locked the house and we disappeared. But before we left, she knocked on uncle's door and shot him six times between the legs and once in the face. She drove all night and day until we arrived in Joburg.

She had read in the newspaper that the police suspected a robbery gone wrong, and that they had killed my uncle during the process. They had transferred the deed of his house to Mom, along with his wealth. Relieved, we could continue with our lives without living in fear or looking over our shoulders.

And we never had to fear him again.

But when Mom died, I couldn't handle her death. It brought back memories of being hurt. I checked myself into a rehab clinic that specialized in trauma and addiction, and after two years I left healthier and free.

When I returned to the same seaside town we had to leave, I brought Mom's ashes with me and had them buried with my dad. And moved into our old home; this home. When she died, it became my home.

But little by little my mind had fractured while I stayed here. I was living in an alternate reality where everything I did wasn't real. I doubted I'd even left the house as my reality shifted into what I'd imagined versus what was real.

It was only when Colin dropped off the package that everything shifted back into place, but only after he tried to kill me; bringing me back to life.

Somehow, what he did had balanced everything out where I could think and see clearly again.

Relief washed over me.

Nothing bad had happened.

And from tomorrow everything would be fine again.

Chapter Twenty-Two

Once I showered and got ready for bed, I paged through the book: *'The Seven Deadly Sins'*.

Now I understood why I'd *killed* all those men. It made perfect sense; I was projecting sins from this book onto them and then *killing* them *in my mind*. But the way I'd killed them was another story altogether. It was so gory and malicious; I would need my head examined for that alone.

I found torn-out pages from the magazines I'd bought; an article for each of the men, and one for a praying mantis; the female insect who killed her partners during sex. That's how I selected them. That's how I killed them. I based the selection on these articles from the local magazine.

What shocked me the most was that it had only been two days.

Two days!

I'd only been in the house for two days, and for two days my mind warped in on itself and made up all these fantasies. I shuddered at the thought.

Colin had recommended a therapist who had medical rooms above the coffee shop. I was seriously considering making an appointment. I needed help.

Yawning, I placed the book on my bedside table, flicked off the lamp and settled under the covers.

Exhausted from everything that had happened during the day, and the realisation that what I had thought I had done was only something I had conjured up. Sleep was a welcome distraction.

As I closed my eyes, a weight rested on my chest, and I struggled for air. My eyes fluttered open, and I saw *his* face.

"Hello my special girl, remember me?" Uncle Keith said through his ghost-like features.

When Mom aimed her gun at his face and fired, it had split his face in two. Then she riddled the lower half of his body with holes until gore and intestines oozed out, with his dick hanging loosely to one side.

I screamed at the sight of the ghost of the man who had hurt me and haunted me my entire life.

And now, he would haunt me still.

Except this time, nobody could rescue me.

Also by SD Syns writing
as Natalie Michaels

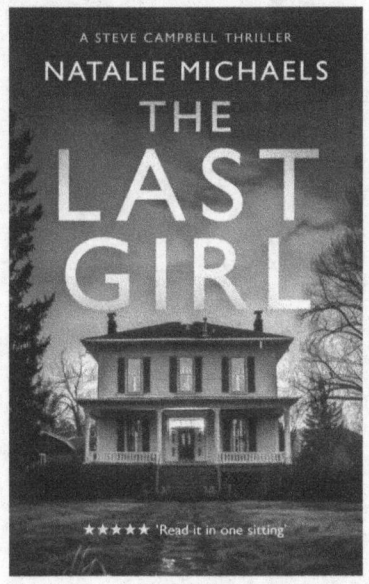

vinci-books.com/lastgirl

Some monsters don't hide—they hunt.

When two women vanish in Ketchum, Detective Steve Campbell
uncovers a chilling link to a predator who's been hunting for years.
As the clock runs out, he must face the darkest corners of Haskins'
lair to save the last girl.

Turn the page for a free preview…

The Last Girl: Chapter One

THE CABIN

Jacob
1987

The quiet evening pierced my ears. Carefully, I climbed out of the water and onto the wooden deck without making a sound. I exhaled silently as I monitored the couple fast asleep in the boat. Tiptoeing on the wooden deck, I was careful not to stand on a creaking plank and when I reached the door, Katie stirred in the boat, mumbling someone's name. I opened the door, testing to ensure it didn't moan the wider I opened it, and slipped out.

I traversed the dark path to the house and entered. Leaving the lights off, I navigated my way around the living room, kitchen, until finally upstairs. I entered the main bedroom and found his suitcase again. Flipping through his wallet, I found what I was looking for and headed back down to the kitchen. Their food remained on the counter, waiting for them to enjoy, and I opened the pantry door.

Once done, I slipped out the front door and found a place hidden in shadows where I could see most of the house and waited. I heard cars driving on the ID-75 entering and exiting Ketchum and was grateful they were a distance away and wouldn't see me or my vehicle from the road.

It was ten at night by the time Katie and her friend staggered up the path, switching on lights as they entered the house and headed for the kitchen. Katie warmed their dinner while her friend sat at the table, waiting for her to serve him.

The itch at the back of my neck started up again, but I didn't scratch. I just rubbed the offending area and waited.

Katie dished food onto their plates and sat beside him. My body heated as I watched him eat. All was fine for a few seconds and then… he grabbed his throat. His eyes widened in horror. Red blotches formed on his face and neck. His face started swelling, along with one side of his neck. He pushed away from the table, stood up, then doubled over as if trying to expel whatever was lodged in his throat.

Katie was there to slap him on his back, but nothing helped.

Nothing would help him.

The man pointed to the stairs and then to his neck. Katie nodded and frantically ran upstairs.

Moments later, she returned, shaking her head. "There's nothing there," she cried.

Shock flashed in his eyes. He collapsed onto his knees, then fell on his chest and face, unmoving.

Katie dashed around, looking for something, but there was nothing that could help him. She fell to her knees and moved him onto his back so she could proceed with CPR, but his throat had already closed, shutting off all his air supply.

From where I stood, his face and neck had swollen to the point where his cheeks were red, round and puffy, and his eyes had bulged. While his fat lips had started turning purple.

After about ten minutes, Katie sat back on her haunches, crying into her hands.

I dropped the epinephrine injection on the ground and crushed it with my boot heel. Pushing through the branches, I approached the cabin with purpose and entered through the front door.

Katie flinched when she saw me and stood up. "Jacob, what are you doing here?" she asked, glancing nervously at me and then at her friend on the floor.

"I thought you might need some help," I said mysteriously and crossed the threshold. My clothing was still damp, and I left wet marks everywhere I stepped.

Katie backed up, glancing at me and the body. "We need to call for help," she stammered, "could you—"

"No," I yelled, shutting her up. "No more, Katie," I snapped. "You've been playing me for years. No more." I pulled the box out of my pocket and placed it gently on the counter. "I've had this for a while, waiting for the right moment to give it to you. To ask for your hand in marriage. Ever since that day in the barn, I've loved you more than anything else. I would've given you the world, anything, and everything you ever wanted. But," I paused for effect and stared into her sad, blue eyes, "you've made it perfectly clear where I stand with you."

The Last Girl: Chapter Two

THE SECOND WEEK IN DECEMBER

Michelle
2001

Jessica combed her long blond hair and tied it in a low ponytail. She fixed her black top; the one I had bought her for her birthday with the famous Rolling Stones tongue. Then she fastened her belt and pulled on her coat. Grabbing her makeup bag, she applied eyeshadow, mascara that made her green eyes brighter, and lipstick sparingly, transforming her youthful face into a more mature look.

We had become best friends since first grade in the Ernest Hemingway School in Ketchum. Since then, we did nothing without the other. Once a month, we visited Mike, our good friend, and went to O'Brian's Pub for a few beers and a couple of games.

"How do I look?" she asked, twirling.

"Like you're twenty-two," I said, grinning. I pulled on my coat and huddled into it. "How about me?"

"Perfect," she said.

I wiped some makeup out of the corner of my eye and smiled. My eyes had thick eyeliner, highlighting my big brown eyes, and I tied my black hair in a low ponytail. I had a fair complexion and with my hair being naturally black; I looked like a porcelain doll. But I was not as beautiful as Jessica.

"Are you two wenches finished?" Mike yelled outside the bathroom. "I'm hungry, and there's a game with my name on."

"Yeah, yeah, we're done," I said, opening the door.

Mike stood in the doorjamb, blocking my way. He wore his signature black outfit; black army boots, black cargo pants, and a long sleeve black vest with a black jacket over. With his brown hair shaved close to his head, he reminded me of someone who should be in the army and not out drinking.

I waved the air in front of my nose. "You smell like weed again."

"I know. You want some?"

"No, thanks."

"Come," Jessica said, pushing past Mike, "there are men who need to buy us drinks."

"You're such a skank," Mike said, chuckling, his smile reaching his light brown eyes. If it wasn't for the gothic clothing he wore, I thought he was handsome.

"You're just jealous you can't get free drinks." She cooed.

"Whatever, now come," Mike said, jogging down the stairs. "Bye mom," he yelled into the lounge. His mom waved and continued watching her fantasy series.

We climbed into Mike's blue van, his Passion Wagon, and drove the short distance to O'Brian's Pub. It was a quaint little drinking hole where a lot of the residents frequented. The place smelled like stale ale. The bar counter was sticky from years of spillage, and the beer flowed all night long.

Mike parked the van in the only available parking spot, which was right at the back underneath the one lamppost that didn't work. We traversed the recently cleared path as snow continued falling around us.

I entered the pub first, and the heat smacked me in the face. Shivering from the sudden change in temperature, I headed for the bar and stood between two men talking about their workday.

"Oh, I'm sorry. Am I bothering you?" I asked, fluttering my eyelashes.

"No, sweetheart," the man on my right said. "But I would love to buy you a drink?"

"A beer will do," I said, smiling sweetly.

"Hey Nancy," said the same man, "get my lady friend here a beer."

"Make that two, please, kind sir," Jessica said behind me.

"Make it two," he said with a wicked grin. "And who might you be?"

"Jessica," she said, holding out her hand for him to shake.

Nancy gave us our beers.

The man stood to retrieve his wallet from his back pocket, paid, and sat down again. Jessica and I stood on either side of him and kissed him on the cheek.

"Thank you," we said together and disappeared into the crowd near the back, where Mike was already playing a game of pool.

We laughed and joked around. We tampered with

Mike's cue stick every time he tried to take a shot, sipped from his friends' drinks, and enjoyed our evening.

I loved coming here, as did Jessica. We were together, we always had fun, and we never had to pay for anything.

"I feel like a shot," Jessica said, swaying slightly.

"You've had enough," I said, slipping my arm through hers. "How about we ask Nancy for something to eat and two glasses of water?"

"Nah, I want a shot." Jessica unhooked her arm from mine and made a beeline toward the bar. She bumped into a man wearing a blue jacket sitting at the bar and started talking to him. She laughed at whatever he said and sat beside him. They seemed to enjoy each other's company and now and then, Jessica would touch his arm or laugh at whatever he said. Then she thumbed over her shoulder at me. But the man didn't turn around.

Mike cut in front of me, blocking my view. "Move," I moaned and pushed past him. When I could see Jessica again, she downed a shot with the man and then he stood up from his stool. He pointed at the door, and Jessica nodded.

"What are you doing?" I mumbled to myself.

"Where are you going?" Mike asked.

"To stop Jessica from making a big mistake."

"She's a big girl. She can take care of herself."

"She's only nineteen, Mike," I grumbled. "We need to look out for each other."

Mike raised his hands in mock surrender. "Fine, but if you aren't here when I'm ready to go, I'll leave your ass here, too."

I rolled my eyes and headed for the door. Jessica and the man had already left by the time I pulled on my coat. I opened the door, and the cold air stole my breath as I braved the chilly night.

A car's engine rumbled to life in the distance, and I turned to look, but couldn't see much. A light came on and I squinted.

"Jessica?" I yelled and headed for the car. "Jessica?" I yelled again, waving my arms so she could see me.

A car door slammed, and a figure headed my way. "Michelle," Jessica said, closing the gap. "I'm going home with my new friend." She wiggled her eyebrows. "I'll see you at Mike's tomorrow," she slurred, hugging me. When she let me go, her now dull green eyes glazed over as she smiled.

"Are you sure you're in condition to go home with anyone?" I asked.

"Relax, I'm fine. Besides, everyone knows him," she said, turning around.

"Who is he?" I asked. There were moments like now when I hated going out with Jessica. She had gone home with guys once or twice before, but I had always met them beforehand. I didn't know who this guy was, and it left me worried.

"It's fine, he's fine, I'm fine," she mumbled. "I'll see you in the morning." She waved over her shoulder as she walked to his car.

"Who is he?" I yelled, but she didn't hear me.

Once Jessica climbed into his car, he turned around, blinding me with his headlights. Once I could see again, all I saw were his taillights in the distance.

I didn't like her going off with some stranger she had only just met and even though he was someone everybody knew, apparently; I didn't know who he was.

Something didn't sit right with me, but I shook off the bad feeling. She was a young adult and could handle herself.

When I went back inside the pub, I had sobered up and asked Mike if we could leave. He handed me the keys and asked me to drive.

Once back at his place, I settled into the bed beside him, and he started snoring; I laid awake with worry.

The next morning, when Jessica didn't come home, I asked Mike to take me to the police station. I waited to speak with an officer, filled out forms, and explained what had happened.

When Monday came and went and Jessica still hadn't come home, and I hadn't heard from the detective, I went back to the police station. They reassured me they were investigating and would give me feedback by Wednesday.

Wednesday passed, and the detective called me on Thursday to let me know they had no leads or witnesses. He also informed me that there were many people at O'Brian's Pub and Nancy didn't remember Jessica or me being there, therefore nobody knew who the man was she had gone home with.

When Friday arrived and I still had heard nothing, I asked Mike to go with me to the pub, but because Christmas was next Tuesday, he was taking his mother to visit his aunt in Sun Valley.

I went alone to the pub, but it was empty, with only a few patrons; none of them remembered me and I couldn't recall them either. I came home early and vowed to go the next weekend and the next until I found out who Jessica's kidnapper was.

If he was local, he had to return.

The Last Girl: Chapter Three

TOUGHEN UP

Jacob - 8 years old
1974

Mama had a headache and didn't join us at church today. Papa told me we had to hurry home because he needed to tend to the sheep.

"I need to use the bathroom," I said, shifting uncomfortably in the backseat.

"We'll be home soon," Papa said, slowing the car as we drove through the town. He waved at Kip and Gladys, who worked at the Ketchum post office. I found it strange they were at work since they rarely opened on a Sunday.

I ground my teeth when Papa went over a bump, rocking the car. "Papa, please, can you stop? I need to use the bathroom."

"Toughen up, boy, we're almost home."

Tears welled in my eyes. Pain erupted in my tummy.

"Oh Jesus, fine, I'll stop at the gas station."

As Papa stopped the car, I bolted out, but I didn't make it to the bathroom in time. I stopped a stone's throw away from the door that led to the men's bathroom. The warm urine ran down my leg, in my shoe, and absorbed into the dry sand.

"Oh shucks," Papa said beside me, "it looks like you didn't make it after all. You can be lucky you didn't do that in my car." He chuckled. "I would've beaten you so badly if you messed in my car."

"Jacob wet his pants. Jacob wet his pants," three boys sang as they passed us on their bicycles. They were from my class and I knew they would tease me at school tomorrow again.

My cheeks heated, and I covered my crotch area with my hands. I glanced up at Papa, who still grinned down at me.

"Come, you've already wet yourself. Might as well climb into the car like that." Papa climbed into his car and started the engine. He glanced over his shoulder, staring at me.

Heat rose into my chest, and neck and I fisted my little hands.

"Move it," he yelled.

I stomped toward the car, opened the door, and climbed inside, slamming the door closed. My cold, damp pants stuck to my skin, making me shiver. I folded my arms across my chest, and I didn't want to look at him.

"You will become a man one day and you need to stand up for yourself," Papa said, glancing at me in his rear-view mirror now and then while he drove. "And one of those things is managing your bladder. You can't go around pissing your pants."

"Yes, Papa," I said, glancing out of the window. Our farm was on the outskirts of Ketchum, a quiet mountain town far from any city, yet close enough that one didn't want to go anywhere. Mountains surrounded our town with crystal clear waterways, hiking, and biking trails, and when it snowed everybody went skiing.

"And you need to stand up to those boys," Papa said. "They're going to bully you."

I didn't want to talk to him anymore, so I continued glancing out of the window, watching the world go by.

We passed the local cemetery where they had buried Ernest Hemingway. Mama had told me a story about the famous author and how he killed himself. They diagnosed him with some disease I couldn't pronounce. His father, sister and brother also killed themselves; I hoped I didn't get what they had.

Papa turned onto the dirt road leading up to our farmhouse and relief washed over me; I could take a nice bath and put on dry clothing. I wrinkled my nose at the smell of my urine-stained pants.

When Papa stopped the car, I climbed out and sprinted up the path toward the house, then stopped when Papa called me.

"Hurry, boy, you have chores to do."

"Yes, Papa," I said, climbing up the veranda stairs. When Papa was no longer looking at me, I bolted through the open front door, slamming it behind me. Then ran up the stairs to my bedroom and peeled the wet clothing from my body, throwing them in the laundry basket.

Hushed voices sounded outside my bedroom door, and then water started running in the bath.

There was a soft knock on my door. "Jacob," Mama said, slowly opening the door. "I've run your bath water."

"Thank you," I said, pulling off my damp underwear. "Sorry," I said, averting my eyes.

"It's ok, my son. Perhaps you should've gone before you left church."

"I wanted to, but Papa said to hurry."

She stared down at me with an expression I didn't understand. "Try harder next time because it will be difficult to clean your shoes." She picked up my soiled clothing and shoes and exited. "Hurry and bathe, your father needs you outside."

"Mama?"

She stopped and glanced over her shoulder. "What is it?"

"Why is Papa so hard on me?" I asked, my bottom lip trembling slightly.

Mama opened her mouth to say something but closed her mouth instead.

"Moira!" Papa yelled from downstairs. "Where's my boots?"

"In the closet near the front door."

"Now why did you move it there."

Mama rolled her eyes. "You left them there, Bill," she yelled.

"Don't talk back to me like that, woman."

"Yes, dear," she said, then turned back to me. "Honey," she started, then stopped as if there was something she wanted to say. "Never mind. Now hurry and be a good boy and go do your chores like Papa wants."

"Ok," I said and ran into the bathroom, slamming the door shut. I washed as quickly as possible, dried, and put on my work clothing. I didn't want Papa yelling at me again today.

The chore Papa had left for me to do was what I hated doing the most; to clean the chicken coop. But once that was done, I sat under my favorite oak tree that stood on a small hill a distance away from the farmhouse.

Papa's sheep roamed freely, grazing everything they could find.

I sat by the tree and watched the sunset. It was the first time this afternoon that I felt better after messing my pants. I felt safer and calmer out here.

Something moved out of the corner of my eye and I glanced in that direction. A wild hare sat staring at me. Slowly, I stood up and approached. The hare waited. I pounced. I caught the hare by its tail with my left hand and dug my fingernails into its body with my right hand.

I gritted my teeth as I applied more pressure. The hare made strange growling hissing sounds as it tried to get away. And I squeezed harder until bones broke.

Once I had secured the hare in my hands, I stood up. With one hand gripping it, I pulled the string out of my pocket and wrapped it around its neck. I tied the knot, ensuring the string was tight, and tied the other end of the string around a tree branch.

I watched the hare suffer while it died. There was something primitive yet satisfying about what I had done. I didn't understand it, only that I enjoyed it and wanted to do it again.

Grab your copy…
vinci-books.com/lastgirl

About the Author

N. Gray is a USA Today Bestselling Author who lives in Cape Town, South Africa, with her daughter and adopted cat named Miss Beans. During the day, she's an analyst and provider profiler for a medical insurance company. At night, she types on her curved keyboard, creating fictional characters some may love and others you may want to kill yourself.

She writes in four genres: urban fantasy, thriller, horror, and paranormal romance.

She now writes under Natalie Michaels for her new thrillers and SD Syns for her new horrors.